# Piece by Piece

Amy Gregory

CONTENTS

Acknowledgments .................................................................. I
Chapter 1 ............................................................................... 1
Chapter 2 ............................................................................. 16
Chapter 3 ............................................................................. 23
Chapter 4 ............................................................................. 34
Chapter 5 ............................................................................. 40
Chapter 6 ............................................................................. 47
Chapter 7 ............................................................................. 57
Chapter 8 ............................................................................. 61
Chapter 9 ............................................................................. 67
Chapter 10 ........................................................................... 75
Chapter 11 ........................................................................... 85
Chapter 12 ........................................................................... 99
Chapter 13 ......................................................................... 111
Chapter 14 ......................................................................... 124
Chapter 15 ......................................................................... 139
Chapter 16 ......................................................................... 147
Chapter 17 ......................................................................... 152
Chapter 18 ......................................................................... 168
Chapter 19 ......................................................................... 180
Chapter 20 ......................................................................... 193
Chapter 21 ......................................................................... 197
Chapter 22 ......................................................................... 208
Chapter 23 ......................................................................... 215
Chapter 24 ......................................................................... 223
Chapter 25 ......................................................................... 232
Chapter 26 ......................................................................... 240
Chapter 27 ......................................................................... 248
Chapter 28 ......................................................................... 257

Chapter 29 .................................................................................. 265
Chapter 30 .................................................................................. 287
Chapter 31 .................................................................................. 298
Chapter 32 .................................................................................. 305
Chapter 33 .................................................................................. 311
Chapter 34 .................................................................................. 316
Chapter 35 .................................................................................. 331

# ACKNOWLEDGMENTS

I extend my deepest gratitude to my beloved Nanny and Papa. Your unwavering support has been my beacon through every storm. Papa, you exemplified true strength and integrity, showing me the essence of manhood. Nanny, your boundless love and authenticity have shaped me into the person I am today.

To my dear mother, your steadfast presence in my life has been a source of immeasurable comfort. My love for you knows no bounds.

To my cherished husband and children, your unwavering encouragement fuels my wildest endeavors. Your acceptance allows me to embrace my true self, and for that, I am eternally grateful. You are the guiding light in my darkest moments.

A special acknowledgment goes to Momma O, whose wisdom has been a guiding force since my youth. Your counsel has been a lifeline during my toughest trials, and I am profoundly thankful for your influence in my life.

Lastly, to my beloved companions, Bowser and Rip, you were more than just dogs; you were my faithful companions and reflections of loyalty and love. Until we meet again, my beloved boys.

**NATIONAL DOMESTIC VIOLENCE HOTLINE: 800-799-7233**

**Text START to 88788 or visit www.thehotline.org for support.**

PIECE BY PIECE

# CHAPTER 1

The snow is coming down so thick we can't see two feet out from the headlights of his old, rusty, two-toned Ford pickup. The vehicle is sliding here and there a bit as we make our way from my house to his. Most would find this to be a bit scary, driving in this weather, especially at 14 years old, but not me. Nothing can scare me when I am with him. He is my safe place, the only person who makes me feel truly safe.

At 14, I was still naive and shy, but I knew what I wanted, what I needed: him. Those beautiful blue eyes and only half smile of his made me melt every time. Tall, muscular, with blond hair—he was the poster child for the high school football heartthrob. I don't think he realized it, though, which made him that much more attractive.

# PIECE BY PIECE

I always ride in the middle of the bench seat, just so I can stay as close to him as possible. God, how he smells so damn good and feels even better. How did such a small, plain, awkward girl like me land a guy like him?

During the drive, I think back on how we met. A freshman trying to learn my place in the high school jungle. I thought I was cool when a group of sophomore girls asked me to hang out with them at lunch. A few I knew from band class, but never was I invited to sit with them till then.

I didn't really fit in with girls in general. I was a tomboy to my core. A guy's gal, dressing up in my stepdad's AIR FORCE clothes and running around the woods with the boys. Playing football, kickball, and just about any other sport. More comfortable in jeans, boots, and a t-shirt with my hair up than being in a dress and doing my hair. Make-up was out of the question unless you counted chapstick; cherry chapstick.

*Then*

Excited for lunch, I hurried from class to my locker to get there as fast as I could. Greeted with smiles and waves, I felt better about myself than I had in a very long time. I took my seat in the middle of the group; we started eating our lunch, talking about how awful certain teachers were, and getting excited about the upcoming basketball game.

Sharon, a girl from my band class, turned to me and said, "Hey, so I, um, have a question. I, er, mean a favor to ask you."

I looked around, and they were all staring at me. "Um, okay? What?" I replied shyly, not sure what to expect; I did not trust girls.

She grinned, "Would you please go tell this guy in my class that I have a huge crush on him?"

The way she said it made her sound confident and not scared or worried at all.

"Really? Why can't you?"

The group burst out laughing. I didn't get what's funny about that, but okay.

She giggled, "Oh, Anna! It's just that you have no issues talking with guys at all. It doesn't seem to phase you. So, telling him for me wouldn't even affect you other than maybe it being an inconvenience."

She wasn't wrong. "Wouldn't it be better coming from you, though?" I was seriously confused.

Sharon rolled her eyes as the girls continued to giggle, "Yea, right! What if he says no? Then I am mortified in front of everyone." Her eyes pleaded with mine.

I rolled my eyes. "Yea, sure, whatever. I guess I could."

She squealed, and I was reminded why I did not get along with girls.

"Oh, thank you, Anna! Can you go right now?" She asked, grasping my arm.

"I guess, get it over with. Who is it?"

She pointed to a group of five boys standing at the top of the stairs that led from the lunch room to the gym.

"You see that tall blond with his back to us?" She asked, practically bouncing up and down.

I obviously couldn't see his face, but I recognized a few of the guys he was with.

"What is his name?" I asked as I began to rise from my seat.

# PIECE BY PIECE

"Christian C'Rion," she told me as I started to walk away.

"Thank you, Anna," she practically sang. *Yea, you're welcome, whatever.* I thought to myself as I made my way to the group.

I walked up the steps towards the group. He was a lot taller up close than from where I had been sitting and had to stand on tip-toe just to tap above the middle of his back. By that point, all the guys in the group around him were looking at me. I could tell they were curious as to why I was just walking up alone, to them as I belonged there. Easy, guys, I don't give a crap about your conversation, I thought. I tapped on his arm since he was a step above me, and I couldn't reach his shoulder.

That was when I felt everything went in slow motion. Christian turned around to see who tapped him. He looked me up and down, and then this slow half grin spread across the most gorgeous face I had ever seen. *Since when do I think that about a guy?*

"Can I help you?"

Damn it, even his voice was beautiful. What was in the water where he lived to grow something this pretty? What the fuck, Anna, I thought to myself. *Focus. Great, I am focusing on his mouth.*

"Um, yea, are you Christian O'Rion?"

He broke into a full smile. *Damn it all to hell. How can a smile make him even more gorgeous?* I thought.

"Why yes, I am. And you are?" he said in a voice that made me get chills. *What did that mean?*

"Oh, that doesn't matter. I am just here to tell you, Sharon, over there," I said, throwing my thumb behind my shoulder in her direction, "has a crush on you and is afraid to tell you herself for some reason." I rolled my eyes, "So, I was sent to make sure you knew."

Christian did not even look in their direction. In fact, he never even broke eye contact with me. When I say blue eyes, I mean crystal blue. The kind that reminds you of a gorgeous ocean with white glaciers. You cannot stop looking into them. He said nothing. The guys started to snicker.

"So there, I did it. You know. So, I am going back to the table." I waved at Dominic, a friend of mine, and started to turn away.

"Wait," Christian said.

I turned back. He cocked his head to the side as if trying to gauge my reaction and eyed me up and down again. "Why?" he asked.

"Why what?" I asked back.

"Why did she send you? Why didn't she come tell me herself?"

I could not look away from him. *What the hell is wrong with me?* I thought. "Yeah, I have no idea," I said as I shrugged my shoulders, "you would have to ask her that on your own, bud."

I tried to make light of it because his eyes were so intense I felt he could see through me, see all my dark secrets, and that they were there. Big, dark, mean secrets that I kept hidden. Why couldn't I walk away? Why did I not want to walk away?

"Will you tell her something for me?"

I sighed, "Sure, I'll be the middle man this one time, but y'all are gonna need to talk to each other if this is going to work."

His grin got bigger, and my heart stopped. It's a real thing that hearts stop when you see someone so beautiful you can't think straight.

"Tell her I appreciate it, but I have a crush on someone else."

*Great, just great. Now I get to go tell this girl and listen to high school theatrical dramatic my-life-is-ending bullshit from her'.*

"I guess, but she will want to know who, and I am not making a second trip up here for that," I responded.

Christian's eyes bore into mine. *When did it get so hot in here?* My body got liquid hot. *What the hell is going on?* He licked his gorgeous lips. *Is there not something on him that is not beautiful? I can't see any.*

"Tell her it is none of her business, but if she must know, it is you," he said it so matter-of-factly that I was not sure I heard him right.

"Wait. What? You do not even know me or my name. I did not even tell you my name," I stammered.

The group of guys laughed. He didn't blink, "I want to know you, Anna."

***

"What are you thinking about?" And I snapped back to reality, riding next to him in a snowstorm in his truck.

"Oh, just about how we met," I responded. I lay my head on his shoulder, and he kisses my forehead. I love it when he does that.

"Anna, are those girls still giving you shit?" Christian asked, referring to Sharon and her friends. Ever since that day, they had laughed at me, pointed, and made fun of me, but only if Christian was not around. If he was with me, he would shut it down with just a look.

"Nothing I can't handle. But no, it is not that." He wrapped his arm around me, pulling me closer.

"Then what, baby?" I do not know which is sexier: him calling me Anna in that voice or baby. Probably both are equal.

"Just thinking about how as soon as I saw your face, I knew I was in trouble," I said with a teasing nudge. He pulled me in tighter.

"Yea, well, that makes the two of us," he replied. I grin and giggle.

We pulled into his driveway beside the house. The snow covered everything, but that bright back porch door light shined like a beacon calling me home, which is something I never felt I had. Growing up in a split family in which both parents remarry and have kids makes one feel like an outsider. But for me, it was worse. Having to move every few years because of my stepdad's job made me feel even more isolated. Add in the fact that my biological father was more like an annoying older brother at times and nowhere near reliable; life for me was always depressing and lonely until Christian and his family came into my life.

We came into the house, and the warmth took over me like a blanket. We took off our shoes and coats. He took my hand, leading me into the kitchen. There, at the island, was Christian's mom, Mrs. O'Rion. Although much shorter than her son, Mrs. O'rion had the same gorgeous eyes, hair, and smile.

## PIECE BY PIECE

"Hey, my sweet girl! How are you?" She beamed as she hugged my neck.

I hug her back with a huge grin on my face. *Home is what this hug feels like.* "I am okay, Mrs. O'rion. How are you?"

"Anna, I have told you, call me Diane or Mom."

I grinned shyly, "Yes, ma'am."

Christian took me to his room, where we spent almost all our time when we were at his house. "Mom! Let us know when dinner is ready!" He shouted as he shut his door.

I stood there in the middle of his room, shy but excited. Slowly, he walked up to me, his 6'2," built-like-a-linebacker body towering over mine. He framed my face with his big, strong hands. "Look at me, Anna Lee," he whispered. I do as he says, and I am taken aback by the look in his eyes. Even at fourteen and naïve, I could still see what that look meant. He kissed me softly, his thumbs tracing my cheeks. A small whimper escaped me, and he pulled back but did not let go. My hands found his hips, and I held on for my life. He smelled like a dream and tasted even better.

## PIECE BY PIECE

"You know how beautiful you are?" he asked. It is not really a question, and I know this. I try to look away, not used to compliments, just insults. "Oh no, you don't, Anna. Look at me and listen, okay? You are beautiful, and I will spend every moment I can proving it to you." I didn't say anything. I just pulled him closer to get lost in his kiss. Quickly, our kiss deepened, and I felt his tongue brush mine. I wrapped my arms around his neck, and he lifted me up against his body like I weighed nothing. My legs wrapped around his waist as he carried me to his bed. Laying me down gently, his body covered mine. I welcomed the weight on me; it was my safety blanket.

We had not had sex. I was still not ready. I wanted to wait till marriage, but I was not immune to my strong need for him, even if the feeling was alien to me. Sure, I had been kissed before Christian, but that was it. Nothing further than that till him.

Christian was patient and never pushed me to go further than I wanted to. It was not something we have discussed either, though. *Maybe we should?* Even with his reputation as a player, he had never led me to believe he was. His actions certainly did not show it.

He pressed his hips deeper against mine, and I could feel just how turned on he was. It was new to me, but it also turned me on that I could do that to him. His hands stayed outside my clothes, but I could still feel the heat and electrical pull as if we were skin-to-skin. *Oh, how I want him to be my first, my only.* Thinking about it scared and excited me. *Not tonight, though. I am not ready.*

I rolled him over so that I could straddle him. My waist-long brown hair covered our faces like a veil. "I love your hair, Anna. So gorgeous, like you," he said as he pulled me down against him for some more kisses. I kissed his neck, running a trail of kisses from his collarbone to his mouth.

"You're killing me, Anna!" I smiled against his mouth. His hands found their way under my shirt. I gasped at the feel of his hands on my bare skin.

"Shhh, I won't go any further than you want me to."

"It's not that, Christian."

"Then what is it, baby?" he whispered against my neck. *Damn him.*

"You feel so damn good it's scary," I whispered back.

A knock at the door stopped us. "Christian. Anna. Supper is ready," his mom called through the door. "Okay, Mom! Be right there." He gave me a quick hard kiss and smacked my ass, "Come on baby, I am starving, and since I can't have you, I will just have to settle for dinner." I giggled and shoved him playfully.

We washed up and met his mom, dad, and sister at the table. Christian's dad was a quiet man. Not much to say, but he had kind eyes. You could see how much he adored his wife and kids just by his eyes. *'What is that like? To have a father who cares, a father who loves you?'* I did not know. I had no idea what that was like. Mr. O'Rion gave me a quick grin, and we ate, discussing school and sports till we finished the meal. I helped his mom clean off the table, but she shooed me away when I offered to do the dishes. "Anna, you are the guest, my sunshine, go!" I grinned and went to Christian.

I know exactly where he was so I go straight to his room. He was at his computer looking up music. I quietly shut the door. "What are you up to?" I asked as I wrapped my arms around his neck and looked at the screen.

"Sing this for me, Anna," he said as he played Allison Krause's version of "When You Say Nothing At All." I panicked and dropped my hands, "What? Sing?"

# PIECE BY PIECE

He got up and made me sit on the chair he was just in, "Sing, Anna." I started so quietly that he bent down in front of me and took my hands. '*I cannot sing for shit! Why am I doing this?*' It is because I could not tell him no; he had full power over me, over my heart.

The song ended, thank God, and Christian kissed me. "I love to hear your voice," he said, and I blushed. The next song comes on, Lonestar's "Amazed." He put his arms around my waist, and we began to dance. So slow but so perfect. Just the two of us, kids, really, dancing in his dark room. "I love you, Anna."

I leaned closer to him. "I love you too, Christian, more than you'll ever know."

PIECE BY PIECE

## CHAPTER 2

Every time either of those songs comes on, I am taken back to that night, even after 20 years. Sometimes, the pain of those songs is so great that I have to turn them off. They break my heart every time. That was the night I fell in love and knew what it was like to actually be loved, truly loved, and to feel 100% safe for the first time in my life. The flood of memories from that night rush back to me, slamming into my heart like ocean waves against rocks; dark and violent. Will I ever recover? Will I ever be able to heal? I can feel my anxiety attack coming on and I quickly grab a cigarette from the pack in my car door. No one needs to know how upset 0 am, or why. Especially my children who are in the backseat, or my husband, who is the one driving.

"Why do you always turn that song off?" He asks me.

## PIECE BY PIECE

"Just not a fan of it," I lie. My girls' laughter pulls me out of my racing thoughts. At ten and three years old, they remind me every day how even one choice can change the path of your life, forever. Had I made that choice differently, would these girls be his? Would we even marry?

The war in my head is giving me a migraine. Why do I do this to myself? I am married to an amazing man who I love very much. We have two beautiful girls and a life many would envy. What's that saying? "You never forget your first love." More like, can't forget. That one choice that changed the direction of my life forever. Of course, I can never forget.

From the backseat, my oldest, Danielle, or Dee, for short, says "Mommy there is a boy at my school who likes me!" I glance at my husband, who stares straight ahead, face turning red and knuckles white on the steering wheel. I laugh, "Dee, you're too young for that," I respond. Dee lets out a big sigh that is more like a growl, "Ugh! Mom, I know! I told him he was dumb." My husband grins. "That's my girl," he says all too happily. "Mommy, I like boys!" My three-year-old, Jessie, yells. We all burst into laughter, reminding me that the choice I made led me to this moment.

*Then*

# PIECE BY PIECE

"I don't want to take you home, Anna," Christian whispered as we lay in his bed, holding each other. "Me neither, Christian," I whispered back. Reluctantly, we got up to head back to my house. House, not home. That place was never my home. When we stepped out of his room and went to the living room, I said goodbye to his parents.

We got in the truck and made our way through the snow. The roads were terrible, so we took our time. That made me nervous. If I was even one second late, my stepdad would have flipped, no matter the reason. I wrung my hands in my lap and bit my lower lip, thinking about the consequences. "What's wrong?" Christian asked, interrupting my thoughts. "Nothing," I said, looking out the window.

"I know you better than that, Anna." His eyes were serious.

"Just thinking how Bud will be if we are late." I said quietly.

Christian instantly tensed, his instant anger obvious. Christian hated Bud and Bud hated Christian. A lot. "I'm sorry," I mumbled.

## PIECE BY PIECE

Christian took my hand, kissing the back of it. "Anna, do not ever be sorry when it comes to him. He is a dumbass and I hate that you live in that house with that man and his piece of shit son."

"You and me both."

Christian didn't know the full extent of my hate and anger for Bud and his son, Jack, who happened to be in Christian's grade.

"You will tell me if they say or do anything to you, especially Jack, right?" His voice was so serious, it was scary. "Yes," I said.

"Promise me, Anna."

"I promise."

I hated lying to him, but I couldn't tell him the truth. *If he ever finds out, I don't know what he would do,* I thought. I did find it funny though, just how scared of Christian Jack is. I used it to my advantage when I could.

"When the snow is gone, we can take the Chevelle out," Christian said, changing the subject. The 1969 Chevelle was almost as gorgeous as he was. Black on black with a 350-

horsepower turbo-jet 396 v8. I knew that only because Christian loved that car more than his own life. He and his dad worked on it for a few years before his 16th birthday so it was ready when he got his license. Everyone at school loved that car and I could not wait for him to take me to school in it.

We pulled up to my house five minutes late. Christian walked me to the door and kissed me good night. The front door swung open and there was Bud. He was just a hair shorter than Christian. He puffed out his chest and stood rigid to make himself look bigger than he was, trying to be intimidating, when in reality he looked like an idiot. "You are five minutes late, girl," Bud said, glaring at Christian. Christian squeezed my hand and looked around casually before he replied, "With the current state of the roads, I would say we are on time. You wouldn't want me to hurry and risk a wreck, would you, Mr. Evans?" He annunciated the Mr. because he knew it made Bud angry.

Right on cue, Bud's face got red and he gritted his teeth. Without looking away from Christian, Bud said, "Get in the house, girl. Now." I started to go inside but Christian pulled me back, kissing my forehead, "I love you Anna, don't forget." I smiled shyly, "I love you too." I snuck past Bud and saw his hands bawled into fists. "Better get home, boy, roads are getting worse. Be a shame if you wrecked." Christian saluted Bud, looked past him, and winked at me. I tried not to laugh.

Bud slowly closed the door and followed me up the stairs where our kitchen and living room were. My mom, Jack, and my two little sisters, Rhea and Josie, were all sitting in the living room. "Hey baby, how was Christian's?" My mom asked me. "Good, his mom made a great dinner."

"What else did you do?" Bud demanded from behind me. I instantly tensed, going on alert mode. *Uh-oh.* From across the room, Jack grinned arrogantly. *Shit, not good.* Without turning around, I responded, "We watched a movie and talked." I heard Bud snicker, "Yea right." I whipped around to face him, defensive and mad.

"Anna...." My mom cautioned. *Fuck this.* I was so sick of Bud and Jack's arrogance and their need to control me. "What's the pig snort supposed to mean, Bud?" I said, glaring at him.

He crossed his arms over his chest, "From what I am told, you have become his little whore."

"And where did you hear that?" I spat venomously. I was shaking.

## PIECE BY PIECE

"Doesn't matter because I know it is true." He sneered.

"How? Because you were there? Or because Jack told you?" I turned to Jack. "How would you know when you know nothing about sex? You're scared of your own hand." Jack got up angrily. Before he could respond, I was hit hard from behind. I turned to see Bud in my face, towering over me.

"Bud!" My mom screamed, but she did not so much as even stand up from her chair. Rhea and Josie sat quietly, faces down.

"You will have more respect for me and your brother, girl! You fucking hear me?"

"He is not my brother!"

Again, I got slapped across the face. "You think because you're Christian O'Rion's whore now that you are tough? Something special? Open your eyes, girl! He is using you! You are his plaything till the next one comes along."

I ignored him and ran downstairs to my room. I shut the door, fell into my bed, and burst into tears. I could already feel the bruising on my face.

# CHAPTER 3

*Now*

I sit on my deck, overlooking our private lake. We are surrounded by woods and I would not have it any other way. I love nature. The less people, the better. Kind of funny, considering my profession is to work with multiple people a day. It is early morning; Rafe has already left for work. I use this time to enjoy the quiet and a cup of coffee with a cigarette before I have to wake the girls up and get them ready for school.

The nightmares are back. I hate them so much. Even after 13 years since Bud's death, he haunts my dreams more times than I care to think about. In the recent dream, he stood over me while I lay on the ground covered in blood. He had a smug smile on his face as he pointed the gun. I looked around for help, knowing there was no one. There never is. I turned back but this time it wasn't Bud, it was Christian. "Why, Anna?" He said sadly, my heart breaking. The sound of the gun going off in my dream was enough to wake me, shaking with cold sweat. Rafe, asleep next to me, did not even stir. The man could sleep through a hurricane.

Trying to shake the feeling of reliving my dream, I take a sip of the coffee and then get on social media. I am friends with Christian, but we never acknowledge each other. He doesn't really post anything much. I am also friends with his mom. We comment on and like each other's posts and chat every now and then. I miss her so much. Every time Christian gets a new girlfriend, my heart breaks. The most recent one has moved in with him. Why do I still care? I am happily married! Admittedly, part of me is secretly happy that he is not married and has no children. I think that would destroy me more than I already am. We have not spoken in 14 years. I haven't seen him in 14 years. So, why do I care?

I reflect on my life and thank God for all that I have. Two beautiful girls, a job I love, and the most amazing husband who taught me to love and trust again. We have been through hell and back. Rafe is strong in every way. His patience with me is that of a saint. I need to let go of my past, but I don't know how. Maybe I just can't let myself let go.

*Then*

I woke up the next day to faint bruises on my face. A little make-up and no one would know, not even Christian. *If he ever finds out, he will kill Bud and Jack. He can never know.*

I finished getting ready for school and headed upstairs to get my chores done before the bus came. I could ride to school with Jack, but I was not in the mood for his shit. Bud had already left for work, thank God. Funny, I didn't even think there was any God, how could there be? What God would allow this to happen to kids? But I still thanked him.

My mom was getting ready to walk out the door. "Hey Mom, have a great day," I said as I went towards the kitchen.

"Anna, can we talk quickly?" She asked.

"Sure mom, what's up?" I turned on the stairs to face her. The look on her face told me she was unsure how I would respond, so I instantly got defensive. I felt my body tense up and my heart race.

"Are you sleeping with Christian?"

It took me a few seconds to register what she had just asked me. I sighed, "No Mom, I am not sleeping with Christian, or anyone, for that matter. Contrary to popular belief, I am not ready and have never had sex."

She stared at me, gauging to see if was lying. "It's just, well, I know his reputation and even though his parents are great people, he is bad news. I am worried about you."

I instantly got pissed. "Reputation? Seriously, mom? I am not stupid, okay? I can take care of myself! I have been pretty good at it since I was 4!"

She flinched like I hit her. "What is that supposed to mean?" Her tone changed to anger.

I rolled my eyes, which just pissed her off more. "You know exactly what I mean or you wouldn't have reacted like I hit you. I have no one to look out for me, protect me; it has been that way since I was 4 years old." Her face got redder with each word. Behind the anger, I could see the pain. I hated hurting my mom's feelings, but I needed to speak up about that matter.

"Your attitude is out of control, Anna! Stop being so damn dramatic! You blame him for everything, and nothing I do is good enough for you! I am sick of it! If it wasn't for Bud, you wouldn't even have a dad!"

I went down the stairs and stood toe to toe so she could see my face. I pointed to my cheek, "This is what dads do, Mom? This is how he shows he cares for me?"

She turned and grabbed her purse, "I don't have time for this, I'm going to be late to work."

I followed her as she walked to the door, "Of course, you don't have time for this, you never do, you're just going to pretend nothing happens, that he doesn't hit us!" I was practically spitting and seething.

"You know what, Anna, maybe if you would keep your mouth shut and think of others before yourself, he wouldn't have to hit- uh, discipline you." I stopped cold. *No way did she just say that.*

I nodded, "Oh, okay, I see how it is. Have a great day, *Mom*." I turned and went upstairs to do my chores as the door slammed behind me.

I got to school and headed to my locker where Christian found me. "Hey baby," he said as he kissed me. My mood instantly changed. I could physically feel myself relax; I was safe. He walked me to my first class, passing Sherry and her friends in the hall. I looked at the ground to avoid eye contact, but I could still hear them.

"What a slut!"

As they pointed and laughed. Christian gave them a look that could stop a train. "Even if Anna wasn't here, you would not have a snowball's chance in hell with me, Sherry. I suggest you stop now, jealousy does not look good on you." He directed his attention to her friends, "Don't forget, I know things about each of you that I am sure you do not want the entire school to know."

I stood behind him, my hand secure in his big one, his body guarding me. I couldn't even see over his big shoulders and I was okay with that. *Damn, he is sexy as hell.*

"Have a great day, girls." With the bitter words, he pulled me away, wrapping his arm around me. His warmth was like a safety blanket. "You, okay?"

I shrugged, "Yes, thank you. You didn't need to do that." I said shyly, looking at the ground as we walked.

He stopped me, "You are mine, Anna. I will always protect you from anything and anyone. No one hurts you and gets away with it, do you understand?" I nodded. *Exactly why you don't* know about Bud and Jack, I think to myself. "I will see you at lunch, okay?" He said as he kissed me and the bell rang. "I love you, Anna, never forget."

I smiled, "I love you too, my hero." He gave me his amazing, sexy grin with his crystal blue eyes glittering.

"Get a damn room!" My friend, Dom, jokingly said, walking up to us.

"Shut up, Dom," I laughed. He high-fived Christian.

"I'll watch her, bro," Dom said to Christian as he pulled me into class. When I moved to town in 4th grade, Dominic was one of my first friends. We went to birthday parties, played football, and were always each other's partners for gym class when we had to square dance. Dom was the "it" guy in my class. He did have a Patrick Swayze look to him. The girls fell over their feet for him, but I saw him as a big brother and a great friend.

I sat next to my best friends, Alex and Lisa. "How's the life of being Christian's girlfriend treating you?" Alex asked wiggling her eyebrows. I rolled my eyes and laughed. Inseparable since we met, Alex and Lisa knew me better than most.

"It's good," I grinned.

Lisa eyed me quietly, "How is Bud handling this?" Lisa knew about Bud, and so did Alex. They had witnessed his temper with me.

"As good as a dumbass who just figured out he is a dumbass, I bet," Alex said.

"Pretty much," I replied right before class started.

*Now*

I sit in my therapist's office, thinking back on my life. "Anna?" He says, "You're staring into space. Want to tell me what you're thinking so I can help you with it?" I smile. After 15 years and multiple therapists, I found the one that has truly helped me, does not sugarcoat things, or constantly ask, "How does that make you feel?"

I sigh, "My nightmares are back," I say. My therapist, Todd, waits for me to continue. I play back my nightmare for him. He takes a second to absorb what I told him.

"Sounds like you're still holding onto the past; holding on to the regret, anger, resentment," he tells me. All I can do is nod. *How do you just let go of 18 years of trauma?* "It won't happen overnight, Anna," he continues, as if reading my mind. I nod again. "You need to hand over your past to God. Let Him heal you. I know you do not feel worthy of God's love and forgiveness," I go to say something and he holds his hands up to stop me and continues, "But you are. For your own mental health, you need to forgive them all. And take Christian off the pedestal you keep him on."

I make sure he is done before I respond. "I hurt him so badly. He did nothing to deserve what I did, regardless of my reasons for doing so." I hold back tears. *Fuck, why do I always cry when I relive this?*

Todd purses his lips, thinking, tapping his fingers on his desk. "Anna, Christian is not innocent, either. What he said and did to you, that is on him, not you." Easy for Todd to say. Christian would never have acted that way, had things gone differently. "Have you thought about telling him everything?"

I swear my heart stops, "Tell Christian? Now?"

Todd nods, "Yes Anna, you said you were friends on social media, right?" Todd says with a tone that tells me to quit playing dumb.

"I can't do that," I stammer.

# PIECE BY PIECE

"Why not?" He retorts, waiting for my answer.

"Because it was 20 years ago. We don't speak or interact on social media at all. I haven't seen him in person in 12 years! What do I do? Just message him out of the blue like oh hey, Christian, remember that time I stomped on your heart? Well, after 20 years, I have decided to tell you the full truth about it?" Tears are rolling down my face.

Todd hands me a tissue before replying, "Is it talking to him again that scares you or is it having him know the truth and not care?"

I chew on my bottom lip, "Both."

"Okay, my next question is that had you made a different choice 20 years ago, what do you think would have happened? How would you see that playing out for you?"

Trying to lighten the mood, I sarcastically respond, "That's two questions, Todd."

"Then answer them both, Anna."

*Damn, so much for lightening the mood.* I sigh, "Okay. I think Bud would have followed through and I would still have lost Christian and his life would have been ruined."

# PIECE BY PIECE

Todd nods and checks his watch, "Well, time is up for now. Same time next week?"

I stand and smile, "Of course."

# CHAPTER 4

*Then*

It was a home game tonight; girls' basketball. I loved the game. Luckily, the guys did not have a game that day so Christian could watch me play. He sat in the stands with my mom and his mom. I thanked God silently that Bud was not there. I hated it when he came to anything I did. I was constantly in some sort of extracurricular activity to stay out of the house and away from him and Jack. *Fucking pricks.*

Ever since Christian and I got together, many of the girls started hating me, more than usual. A few played on the team with me but we did not interact unless we were playing and we had to. During warm-ups began, Stacy shoulder checked me, hard. "Oops. Sorry, slut," she said to me with mocking laughter.

# PIECE BY PIECE

I ignored her. She wanted a reaction but she wasn't going to get it from me.

Coach called us all back to the bench before the game started. "Alright girls, I am changing the starting lineup. I need Emma, Tracy, Brook, Liz, and Anna."

Stacy jumped to her feet, "Coach! What the hell? I thought I was starting! You told me that!"

Coach shrugged her shoulders, "Sorry. Maybe next time you will be a better team player and then you can start."

Stacy turned to me hysterically. "This is all your fault!"

Coach cut in, "You want to take a seat in the stands instead of the bench?"

Stacy glared at me then back at the coach, "No ma'am."

"Then I suggest you take your seat and cheer your team on." She flopped into her seat as I took the court, feeling her death stare. Before I could think too much about it, the game started.

Down by 20 by the end of the first quarter and tied up by half-time., I felt pretty confident. Christian brought me a

Gatorade. "You're amazing out there, babe!" His proud grin did make me feel amazing. The buzzer went off, signaling the second half of the game. I sat on the bench for most of the third quarter, exhausted from the first half. By the fourth quarter, the team had pulled ahead by 4 points. "Anna! Stacy! You're in!" Coach yelled. *Great.* Stacy was still sour after the coach called her out. We went in and within 30 seconds, I got fouled. I was given my two free throws, which were my specialty.

"Better sink them, whore, do not cost us the game!" Stacy spat from her spot. Beth, her best friend, snickered from her position. *Fuck them.*

"You got this, Anna!" Christian cheered from the stands. I grinned at Stacy and Beth. I was pretty sure there was smoke coming from their ears. I lined up, shot, and followed through; nothing but net. The home team bleachers cheered. I lined up a second time, shot, followed through, and it went into the net once again. The crowd went wild and we headed down the court for defense.

I waited for the opponent to come down the court with the ball. I got in my stance; arms out, legs wide, knees bent, butt out. Easily six inches taller than me and thirty pounds heavier, I could see the opponent's arrogance all over her face. She pretended to fake left, but I know better. *This is my game; six years of summer basketball camp would not go to waste.*

She hesitated and I took advantage of it. I was able to get the ball and haul ass to our basket. A three-point was all we needed to win the game. I lined up, shot, and followed through. Before I knew what happened, I blacked out as I hit the floor, feeling like I had been hit by a truck. Confused as pain shot up my arm; excruciating pain. The buzzer sounded. *We won!* The team cheered, but no one came to help me. I stood up and immediately grabbed my arm; it was dislocated.

I started to panic, scanning the cheering crowd for Christian and our mothers. They were on their feet rushing to me. Before they could reach me, Stacy smacked my dislocated arm. "Guess you won't be starting for a while, you little slut." Grinning, she took off as the coach, and my mom, along with Christian and his mom got to me.

The pain was insane. I could feel Christian coming closer even if I couldn't see him yet. "Anna! Are you okay? Let me see!" Christian looked terrified. "Shit! Mom! Anna's arm is dislocated!" The pain made me feel woozy.

## PIECE BY PIECE

"Anna! Anna! Look at me, honey!" My mom said. "Oh God, she's hit her head too! Look at the cut!" I noticed the blood on my jersey and realized why I could not focus. "She needs the hospital," my mom called out in a hurry.

"I'll take her!" Christian said, picking me up immediately. In his arms, I felt better already.

Mrs. O'Rion stepped in, "Son, let her mom take her, okay?"

"I am not leaving her, Mom!" His voice sounded scared,

"Mom..." I whined. I couldn't see her, things were getting blurry. "I am here, baby, let's get you to the hospital."

"Mom, I need Christian..." I said weakly, tears slipping down my face.

"Fuck this, I am going," Christian snapped, quickly walking to the door with my body in his arms. *He is strong; I know I am safe.* I closed my eyes.

"Stay awake, baby, talk to me," Christian said as he rushed towards the parking lot. The cold hit me, but Christian's body sheltered me from most of it. My head rested against his chest; he smelled so good. "Christian, get her in my car, now," my mom said sternly in the voice she used when trying to calm kids down. "I'll hold her the whole way if you just drive," he requested to my mom. "You get your car and meet me there, Christian, she will be okay. I promise." He hesitated. "Now, Christian, I need to get going." Her mom voice rose. He reluctantly put me in the seat and kissed my head, "I love you, Anna. I will be right there, I promise."

My head and arm hurt so bad. We arrived at the hospital. Christian was already there to get me out of the car. He scooped me up and I groaned in pain. "I'm sorry, baby," he said.

They got me into the exam room and he set me on the bed, the lack of his warmth immediately taking over me. Panic set in; I was no longer safe. "Christian! Christian!" I cried out; I couldn't see him with the nurses and doctors surrounding me. "Baby, I am right here, okay?" My mom called to me from the end of the room.

"No! I need Christian!" I started crying, "I just need him!"

"He is in the waiting room," the doctor reassured me as he examined my injuries. A panic attack started to settle in me and I didn't feel the IV until the morphine kicked in. Instantly, I went out like a light.

# CHAPTER 5

My phone rings. Mom. Like clockwork, she calls the same time every day. "Hey Madre," I say, answering the call.

"Hey, hun! How are you?" She says in her cheerful voice. I love hearing the happiness in her voice.

"I am good, busy as usual."

"And my girls?"

"Pain in my ass, per usual," I joke, kind of.

She laughs, "Paybacks are a bitch, aren't they?"

It is my turn to laugh, "Yeah yeah."

# PIECE BY PIECE

"Tell her to get her happy ass out here and bring me my grandbabies!" I hear in the background. The voice was deep and loud. I laugh out loud.

"Did you hear your father?"

"Yeah, I heard him."

My dad, Derek, is my mom's new husband. They got together right before I found out I was pregnant with Dee. He is the father I always wanted. Kelly Clarkson's "Piece by Piece" comes to mind whenever I think about him, it is how I describe him.

"You going to listen to my words, baby girl?" He bellows in that deep voice.

"I am planning a trip soon Dad, I promise," I reply.

"Good, I love you!"

"I love you too, Dad."

My mom takes back over. "How's therapy?" She asks. I close my eyes. This is a very touchy subject and I hear the concern in her voice.

"Making progress, Mom."

"That's great. Um, Anna, there is something you should know." The sudden change in her voice puts me on automatic defense and panic mode. I hate my reaction but I can't help it. *Shit. Shit.*

"What, Mom?"

Silence.

"Mom?" I ask again. This time, I hear her sigh. *Oh fuck, this is serious.* My heart races. "Please don't freak out. I am so proud of your progress, and I would hate for this to set you back," she responds.

"Mom, just tell me please." I try to say calmly.

"Jack was released today." My blood runs cold. *No, no, no, this can't be true.*

"What the fuck, Mom!"

"Anna, please calm down."

"Calm down? Are you fucking serious right now?" I hear her start to cry. *Damn it.* I hate it when she cries.

"He has been asking Josie questions, Anna," she says through tears.

"What kind of questions, Mom?"

"About you." I almost feel like I did not hear her right. "Me?"

"Yes."

Panic, fear, anger. All the emotions I had as a little girl growing up come rushing back with full force. I start to panic worse, looking all around my yard as if he was there. "Josie won't tell him anything, Anna, you know she won't."

My mom tries to reassure me. "I swear to God, Mom, if she does, I will beat her ass!" I feel the panic attack getting worse. I start pacing the deck, lighting a cigarette. "Mom, he will find me. Oh God, the girls! Rafe!"

"I am so sorry, Anna, I just found out. I don't know what to do." The panic in her voice is matching mine now.

"I do," I respond in a voice so calm and cold I almost don't recognize it as mine.

*Then*

Arm in a cast and a nice bruise on my head even two weeks from the injury, I felt like shit. It didn't take long for the gossip train to roll through school. Stacy and Beth "accidently" slammed into me at that game. They said they were trying to hurry to help me but didn't expect me to stop suddenly at the free-throw line, causing them to collide into me. They seemed too damn smug for the "accident," though.

Christian had been amazing those past two weeks, picking me up and taking me home from school. He also walked me to classes and carried my books for me. My mom told me that on the night of the accident, he was so worried. "He must really care about you, Anna. No boy using a girl would act like that. He was so scared." *I am the luckiest girl in the world.*

"What are you thinking about?" Christian asked, interrupting my thoughts. He was taking me home from school again.

"My mom said you looked worried at the hospital."

"I was terrified, Anna, and I could do nothing but wait," he said, taking my hand.

"But you're not scared of anything, Christian," I responded, fully sincere.

His face was so serious. "I was. You are the only thing that scares me, I don't know what I would do if I lost you in any way, Anna."

I squeezed his hand, "You don't have to be, Christian. I love you. You will never lose me." I started tearing up because I knew I meant every word with all of my being. I loved him, full-blown love. I did not feel like some silly little girl with a crush; I wanted to marry him someday and have his kids.

We pulled into the driveway and saw Jack just climbing out of his truck. Christian helped me get out of his car and we all met up at the deck door. Jack had that dumb shit look on his face. "Alex or Liz are the only two allowed to bring you home. Not him. Dad is going to flip…" he didn't get to finish. Christian cut Jack off, "Daddy isn't going to do shit, and if he does, it is your ass, Jack, you understand?" The look in Christian's eyes proved he was not fucking around.

Jack stepped back like a scared puppy who just got caught shitting on the carpet. He was terrified of Christian, even if he tried to act like he wasn't. "Besides," Christian continued, "I do not trust anyone else with her. No one." Jack got the point and stormed into the house. Christian turned to me, "You tell me if either of them gives you shit, okay?" His tone changed from threatening to soothing. "I am serious, Anna."

I nodded. "Okay, Christian, I will tell you." He kissed me, long and deep. *Fuck, he is an amazing kisser.*

"I love you."

"I love you, too." I stayed on the deck and watched him leave, dreading the upcoming confrontation that awaited me inside.

## CHAPTER 6

"Work is kicking my ass," Rafe says as he pulls a beer from the fridge. "Why, babe?" I respond out of habit, though I am not in the right mindset for small talk. I am still reeling from the news of Jack getting out of prison. "Just busy. Lance and I got slammed with shit and of course, Jeremy had to be gone today." I stop listening while Rafe continues. I really can't pay any attention to this conversation. I am an intense cleaner, so I start going through our kitchen with a spray bottle and a rag.

"Anna?" Rafe says. "Hmm?" Is all I can respond. I am about to cry. Damn it! I am an intense crier, too. "Anna!" He says louder. I slam the bottle down. "Yes, Rafe, what!" I instantly regret my outburst and drop my head. "Whoa, babe, what is wrong?" He says, coming around the island to take me in his arms. "Um, nothing, I am fine." He chuckles, "Woman, I have known you 10 years. You're cleaning hard and not listening, what is wrong?" He is right, he knows. I burst into tears and start shaking uncontrollably.

"Shit, Anna, what the hell is going on baby?" He hugs me tighter. In between sobs, I respond, "Its Jack." He goes completely still and tense. Rafe knows all about my past. I told him everything. I promised myself that if I ever loved again like I loved Christian, I would never lie to them or hide parts of myself. Through gritted teeth, Rafe asks, "What about the bastard?" I pull back so I can see his face, not leaving his arms; I am safe in his arms. "He was released today."

Rafe's face goes red, "That motherfucking son of a bitch!" He practically yells.

"Daddy! We don't say that!" Jessie comes yelling, hands on her hips. I would laugh if it wasn't such a serious matter. She looks like a 30-year-old in a little body.

Dee chimes in, "So, who is the M.F. S.O.B?"

Rafe turns to the girls, "That still counts, Dee Dee."

Dee drops her head, "Dang it!"

## PIECE BY PIECE

"We don't say that either, Dee Dee!" Jessie says, hands still on her hips, mom face going strong.

Rafe turns back to me, "We will discuss this when little ears can't hear big things." I nod. Jessie throws her hands up in exasperation, "I give up."

Rafe scoops her up and she squeals, "Never give up, baby doll, not ever." He carries her to the living room, her sweet squeals and giggles flowing through the house. I am pretty sure he was saying that more to me than her.

"Mom?" Dee says, looking at me with an intensity that is beyond her 10 years.

"Yeah, hun?"

"Did someone make you mad? You were crying and cleaning, so you're like, really mad." My sweet Dee never misses anything.

"Yeah baby girl, they did." I try not to lie to my girls, even if it is for their benefit. I was lied to since the day I was born, I won't do that to them. I won't let them know that pain, along with the other pains I was subjected to as a kid.

Her face turns to concern, "Was it Jessie? Daddy? Me?"

# PIECE BY PIECE

My heart breaks. "No, no, baby, you all have done nothing wrong, I promise." I pull her into a hug.

"Okay, well then, what is for supper?"

*Then*

It had been three weeks since I made the hardest choice in my life. I was miserable and devastated. I didn't really sleep and eat anymore either. My grades had started to slip. I was constantly on the verge of tears. Christian went out of his way to avoid me. If I walked down the hall, he would turn and go another way. At lunch, he kept his back to me, even at the opposite end of the cafeteria.

"Damn dude, you look like shit!" Darren, one of my friends, said to me.

"Thanks, asshole," I mumbled back. He was probably my closest guy friend ever, since elementary. Darren, like Alex, did not sugarcoat anything.

"Seriously though, Anna, what happened? One minute you're on cloud nine, in love with Christian and it looked the same with him, but now? Now, he looks at you like you're Satan, that is if he looks at you at all. I mean, there are rumors of course, but I want to hear it from you."

I shrugged and lied, "Just not ready for the kind of commitment he wanted." What else could I say? The truth? Darren would flip out, so I told him what I had been telling everyone who asked.

When I got home that night, I heard Bud yelling from inside. I stopped to listen. *Fuck! He is laying his hands on Josie!* My seven years younger, baby, half-sister whom Mom and Bud had together, was getting abused. She was my baby though, at least that is how I saw it.

I took off running to the door and I heard Josie scream. Even at 90 pounds, I crashed through the door. The bang sound, I hoped, was enough to take the attention away from her and onto me. It didn't. "You fucking little dipshit!" I heard him yell. Josie screamed again and I heard another hitting sound. I cleared the stairs in three steps.

Josie was on the floor, rolled up in a ball. Bud was above her, his belt in his hand. I saw the welts on her arm and leg. Josie saw me and the fear in her eyes would forever haunt me. I lost it and started seeing red. Before he could hit her again, I threw myself over Josie, covering her body with mine. The blow hit my back and fire seared through me. I didn't even make a sound. That was what he wanted; he fed off our fear of him. Josie was trembling under me.

"It's okay, I am here, baby," I whispered to her. I took another hit to the ribs, wincing but still not making a sound. I didn't flinch; I had been conditioned to not react. "You dumbass, this is between me and her!" Bud yelled at me, "Get the fuck out of my way or so help me god!"

I twisted to look up at him, anger pouring from every part of me, "Or what Bud!" I yelled back.

He stopped, looming over us, belt in hand, "What did you say?" His eyes were full of rage.

I stood up, "So help me god what? You will beat me? Again? You'll kill me? Go ahead! God has nothing to do with this! He doesn't fucking exist! But since you brought it up, Bud," I dragged his name out, knowing he hated it, "so help me god, if you ever touch Josie or Rhea again, *I will* kill you."

The look on his face was unreadable. He came at me, belt raised. I didn't even blink. I stared him down, challenging him to continue. "You mouthy little slut…"

## PIECE BY PIECE

"What the hell is going on!" My mom came into the room, yelling. *Thank fuck she is home.* "I can hear you two outside!" She said as she reached the top of the stairs to where we were.

"Your pain in the ass daughter is getting involved in something that has nothing to do with her, again. Thinking she is the adult!"

I snorted. My mom looked at me, "Anna?"

"He was hitting Josie with a belt," I pointed to Josie who was still on the floor, crying. "She was screaming in pain and fear, mom!" I said in hysterics.

"I was just spanking her!" Bud justified, "There you go again, Anna, being dramatic!" If I had a dollar for every time he used that as his excuse to cover up what he did, I could retire by next year.

"What did Josie do, Bud?" My mom asked him, setting down her purse and jacket calmly like nothing happened.

"She was supposed to do her chores and decided to spill my full cup of tea on the carpet. She did it on purpose for making her redo the chores that she fucked up!" He practically whined his excuse.

## PIECE BY PIECE

My rage took over; I could feel the lava rising within me. "Are you fucking kidding me? That warrants you beating her with a belt? She was on the ground! She's seven!" I yelled at him, my hands in tight fists at my side. *I am going to kill him.*

"Anna! Watch your mouth! Go to your room! Josie clean up the tea." My mom demanded.

"I'll do it!" I said as I headed to the kitchen for a towel. Bud grabbed my arm, squeezing tight. "Go ahead, Bud, do it!" I practically spat at him. He squeezed harder before letting go.

After cleaning the tea off the carpet, I went to my room. Josie was already in her room. I sat on my bed, head in my hands. *If there really is a god, why does he let this happen?* Twenty minutes later, my mom came into my room. "Time to eat." She told me.

"I'm not hungry," I replied in a pissed-off tone. I could feel the bruises already, which just made me madder.

My mom sighed, "Anna, you look anorexic, you need to eat."

"Mom, why do you let Bud get away with this?" I asked, showing her the marks he put on me, again.

"Anna, you stepped in when you shouldn't have. He didn't know you were going to do that. He didn't realize-"

"Twice, Mom!" I cut her off, showing her the other bruises.

"Anna, stop it!" She raised her voice. "For ten years you have been trying to do whatever you can to make him look like some monster. I have had enough!" I stared at her in disbelief, like she had just grown another head right in front of me. "Don't look at me like that. You do have a tendency to overreact to everything. Now come out of your room and eat with us, as a family."

I said nothing as I walked past her to the stairs; what could I say? It was obvious she didn't want to believe me. *Some fucking family.* We ate like nothing happened at all. I sat by Josie, keeping myself between her and Bud.

After, I showered and went to bed. I couldn't sleep though. I never could. My earlier thoughts were confirmed. There was no god, or even if he did exist, he did not care about me at all. I heard my door creak open and I switched to alert mode.

"Anna?" I heard Josie's sweet little voice.

## PIECE BY PIECE

I relaxed and sat up, stretching out my arms for her to come to me, "Come on, Jojo, climb in." She ran and jumped into my arms. "You okay? You hurt anywhere?" I asked as I looked her over.

"I'm okay," she whispered back to me. My heart broke. How was it possible for my heart to even be functioning?

"I can't sleep, Anna, I am scared." She told me as she clung to me. "Can I sleep with you tonight?"

I pulled her closer to me. "Of course, here, get under the covers between me and the wall." That ensured that she was safe behind me, away from the door. My body was shielding her in case Bud came in. *I will kill this bastard.*

# CHAPTER 7

My phone rings; it's Josie. *Shit. I don't need this right now.* I answer anyway; she's my baby sister and I couldn't ignore her. "Hey Jojo, what's up?" I say.

"Uh, hey big sis, um, how are things?" I can tell she's worried.

"Fine, how are things with you?" I try to keep the anger out of my voice, she is fragile as it is.

"Did mom tell you, Anna?" She asks so softly I almost don't hear her.

"Yeah kid, she did." I try to stay as calm and neutral as I can. This is not her fault; it has never been her fault. She is sensitive and the slightest change in my tone could send her running like a scared baby rabbit.

"Anna, I swear, I haven't told him anything!" The panic in her voice rises. Why she still has any relationship with Jack is beyond me. I do not understand it at all. It is an unspoken rule that we don't discuss.

"Jojo, it is okay, seriously. Nothing I can't handle, you know that," I say, trying to reassure her and myself.

Rafe walks into our room where I am pacing. He mouths, "Who is it?" And I mouth back, "Jojo." He sits on the bed, his face giving away nothing.

"There is more, Anna. More that I didn't tell Mom." *Son of a bitch.*

"Okay, what is it?" I ask.

She begins to sob, "Jack says one way or another he will find you, with or without my help." I stop pacing and face Rafe. "Anna, I am so sorry, I tried reasoning with him. I even begged him! But he-"

I cut her off. "Don't you dare beg that piece of shit, Josie. Do you hear me?" I say as I start shaking. "I can handle him. You know it, I know it, and he knows it."

She sniffles and says, "I know that and that is what worries me."

"Don't worry about me, okay, just keep me posted if he says or does anything, please."

We hang up and I replay the conversation to Rafe. By the end of it, he is the one pacing the room. "Maybe you and the girls should go stay with your parents till this is over," I say, wrapping my arms around myself.

"The fuck we will, Anna! You are not dealing with this son of a bitch on your own. You're not a kid anymore, you have me. I will protect you and our girls, you understand me?" He says, hands on his hips, the look of a pure, protective, stubborn male. That's where the girls get it, I guess.

"Rafe, if he finds me, I do not want the girls here. They will never know or see anything remotely close to what I did at their age." I try to lower my voice; Dee likes to eavesdrop.

He runs his hands down his face and sighs, "Then the girls go to my parents," he says and I nod. "How do we even know if or when he will show up, Anna?" I stand from the bed and whistle for Bane; I need him. I drop to my knees and wrap my arms around his thick neck, rubbing his head. "He will Rafe," I say, "he can't help himself." I stand and signal Bane to heel.

"Where are you going?" Rafe asks as I grab my jacket. As I head for the door, I answer.

"The gun range."

# CHAPTER 8

*Then*

Winter break had arrived. I hated winter break, spring break, summer break, basically any time off from school. I hated school, don't get me wrong. But I hated being at home more. *Home.* It was never a home, it was hell. I never had a real home. I was born at the Air Force base in Warner Robins, Georgia. My parents split when I was 2 years old and mom remarried Bud, who was a marine and got a job with the government when I was 4 years old. We moved around a lot till we landed in Philipsburg, Montana when I was in fourth grade. It was a very small town, everyone knew everyone, and nothing was a secret. I loved it though, the outdoors side of it all. I preferred to be in the woods than I did anywhere else.

# PIECE BY PIECE

I was sitting on our deck overlooking the pasture behind the house. Two deer stepped out of the woods into the pasture. I watched them for a while, not ready to go inside, even if it was freezing. Jack came out and said, "Mom says you have to come in before you freeze to death." I rolled my eyes at him. *Mom?* She was not his mom; she was mine and Josie's. Jack and Rhea belonged to Bud and his first wife. Rhea and I got along fine and all. We fought like sisters did and I was protective of her, but not to the extent I was of Jojo.

"Hey dumbass, did you hear me?" Jack snapped, "I don't care if you freeze to death, but I don't want to listen to Mom going on about you."

I slowly turned to face him and said, "It must really suck, Jack, huh?" My tone was very condescending. He looked confused, blinking at me. *Figures.*

"What sucks?" He asked.

"To be so ignorant you can't even see just how much of a little bitch you really are."

He snickered. "You're the bitch, Anna."

I gave him a wide grin and said, "Aw, thanks. I am, aren't I? But you are the prison bitch kind. Tell me, Jack, does your ass still hurt or are you used to it by now?" His face went beet red and he balled his fists.

"I am not a fag!" He practically yelled. I rolled my eyes again.

"I didn't say fag, you're just everyone's little bitch, especially Bud's. He commands and you bend over and grab your ankles." I walked past him with a grin, "Oh, and Jack? I would watch your mouth if I were you and not use the term "fag." One day, someone will beat your ass for it."

His face looked like he was going to have a stroke before he said, "You're pushing your luck, bitch, and you don't have Christian to protect you anymore, dad and I made sure of it." I knew he was trying all he could to get me to react.

"I protect myself, Jack, always have."

"We will see," he said. I walked inside, shutting the door in his face.

PIECE BY PIECE

It was the day before New Year's Eve and Lisa called me. "Hey, you got plans tomorrow night?" She asked in her cheery voice.

"No, why?" I asked and she squealed with joy.

"My cousin's having a huge party at his parent's house and the whole school will be there." Her cousins' parents let him have parties all the time, just about every weekend.

"I'll ask my mom and call you back." We hung up and I went to find my mom.

I found her in the living room with Bud. Jack was at the kitchen table, probably trying to figure out which hand was his left and which was his right. *Oh he'll be there a while.*

"Hey, Mom?"

"Yeah, hun?"

"Lisa just called me, she wants me to stay over at her house tomorrow night. Ben is having a New Year's Eve party next door and we were invited."

Jack jumped from his chair, "How were you invited but not me?"

"Yea, um, I am not answering that one truthfully."

"I have heard about these parties, practically drunken orgies," Bud said. I turned to my mom, ignoring him.

"Mom? Can I go? The parents will be there, you can call and ask."

"I don't know, Anna. Bud? What do you think?" She asked him, looking over at him. *Unbelievable.*

He looked at me and said, "You will stay at Lisa's, correct? After the party?"

"That's the plan. Once it's midnight, we go to her house." Bud nodded.

"Dad! You can't let her go!" Jack whined. I swear his voice had a higher pitch than mine.

Bud turned to Jack, "You telling me how to parent, boy?" Jack cowered. *Little bitch.*

"No, sir."

"That's what I thought."

Bud turned back to me and asked, "Your grades are back up?" I nodded. "If you get your chores done on time, then you can go," he says. "But Jack will take you there." I nodded again. Why is he being nice? This is not good, something is up, I thought. Jack fist-bumped the air, "Yes!" This should be interesting, I said to myself and walked away to call Lisa.

# CHAPTER 9

*Then*

We got to the party at about eight and it was already packed. Ben's house was gorgeous. An old plantation style is what I thought when I saw it. The white columns were the size of trees in sequoia national park! Okay, well, maybe not that big, but to a girl who stood five foot tall, they seemed like it. There were beautiful wrap-around decks on both floors. The music was blaring from behind the house.

"Hey! You made it!" Lisa squealed as she hugged me. Jack came around the truck, "He-hey, Lisa, how's it going?" He asked. He had a crush on her for as long as I can remember. She didn't even acknowledge him, "Let's go, Anna." She pulled me to the side of the house towards the back, leaving Jack to do whatever it was he did. He was on his own there.

# PIECE BY PIECE

As we went around the house, the music got deafening. I could see the glow of the fire surrounded by the patio heaters. Patio is an understatement. Half the school student body could fit on it comfortably. There were two kegs to the side of the back door where a group of guys stood. Many of the girls huddled around the fire and heaters, trying to keep warm in the cold. The speakers on the patio were big enough for a football game, "Hit 'Em Up Style" by Blu Cantrell blasting from them.

"Hey, little cuz!" Ben yelled over the music. Giving Lisa a big hug, Ben turned to me. "Hey, adoptive cuz!" He said, hugging me too. "You okay?" He asked me, a look of concern on his face.

"Yeah, Ben, I'm okay. Thank you for inviting me."

"Well, duh! You're family too, but, uh, why did you bring Jack?" He gestured behind me. I turned to see Jack by a group of guys, doing shots. *Damn it.* The guys were cheering him on and laughing. *At* him.

I turned back to Ben and rolled my eyes. "He was my ride, I didn't have a choice."

"Let's hope he doesn't cause any trouble," Ben said.

# PIECE BY PIECE

Lisa and I spotted some friends and made our way to them by the fire. We talked about whatever it was high school girls talk about, giggling. I got picked up from behind and spun around in a circle. Once back on my feet, I turned to see who did it.

"Hey, Anna! Glad you made it, hun!" Dom said. I laughed and hugged him,

"Hey, Dom."

A few guys from our class were with him and we said hello. Rick handed me a drink, "Here," Dom took it, "Anna doesn't drink."

Lisa stepped in, "She might now." She gestured towards the door; we all looked to see Christian coming out of the house.

He was smiling, high-fiving just about everyone he went by. He grabbed a red solo cup and downed it. "Anna," Dom said, "There is something you need to know…"

"Know what, Dom?" I responded, not taking my eyes off Christian. Dom stepped into my view, looking at me with a worried expression. "I knew he would be here, Dom. It's okay," I said, more to reassure myself than him.

"That's not it, Anna. Um, Christian has, um, he has met someone from another school." Dom said, watching me like I was some fragile kitten. Good thing I was conditioned not to react.

I shrugged, "Okay," was all I could say. Dom looked me over and I could tell he wasn't buying it; he knew me too well. "Anna," he said so softly it broke my heart worse.

*Don't react.* I grabbed the drink from Rick who had been holding it and watching that scene from beside me. I downed it without thinking.

"Anna?" I heard Christian say behind me. I turned slowly and smiled the biggest fake smile I could muster.

"Hey, Chris!" I never called him that. He looked hurt.

"I didn't think you would be here, or drinking," he said. He was right; I didn't drink or go to parties. My biological father was an alcoholic. For as long as I could remember, he had been "borrowing" my birthday or Christmas money or pawning my gifts to buy himself alcohol. I told myself I would never be like him. I would never choose alcohol, partying, and sex over my kids.

Before I could answer, a girl who was built just like me and had the same hair color curled herself around Christian like a cat in heat. His arm went around her. She pouted, "Christian, I couldn't find you anywhere." She was practically purring. "Who are your friends, babe?" She said, looking up at him like I used to. Like he was the most perfect thing she had ever seen. She wasn't wrong.

Christian cleared his throat, "Uh, this is Dominic, Scott, Seth, Rick, Lisa, and-" He couldn't even say my name because she cut him off.

"I know who she is," she said, practically hissing with a look of disgust on her face, staring me down. "Stacy has told me all about her. Come on babe, let's go."

Christian looked at me, for what, I didn't know. A reaction? I shrugged my shoulders and grabbed another drink from Seth. "Anna, I wouldn't," Seth said but I ignored him and slammed the straight Jim beam.

I looked at Christian with a grin and said, "Better go, don't want that cat getting her claws out." I grabbed another drink as they walked away.

# PIECE BY PIECE

"Anna! Slow down!" Dom said, taking the cup from me. "Are you okay?"

I giggled. Alcohol had started to work its magic, dark magic. "I am perfectly fine, Dom, get me another drink, please." He handed me another, reluctantly. I slammed it too. I was anything but okay. I was devastated, pissed, and wanted to run away. I wanted to just die. Running away would mean running to somewhere else and I had nowhere to go, and I definitely did not want to go back to Bud's house. So, death seemed like a better option.

Dom and I entered a game of beer pong, or more precisely, Jim Beam pong. By the end, I was shitfaced. I found out that the new girl's name was Brittany, and she made sure that no matter what I was doing, I was able to see her and Christian. She hung onto him, kissed him, and danced like a girl who really wanted that dollar while on the pole, but the pole was Christian. She also made a point of smiling at me. I smiled back, wiggling my fingers at her. I didn't want to let her know it was getting to me.

I needed a bathroom, quickly. I took off into the house and towards the bathroom. After all the whiskey had come back up, I washed my face and looked into the mirror. I didn't even recognize myself. Pale, super thin, faded bruises, and dead eyes. "Get your shit together, Anna," I said to myself as I dried my hands and headed back to the party.

I passed by a bedroom and heard Lisa's voice say, "Anna, in here!" I followed her voice and saw her and a few others around the T.V. playing mortal combat. "We're having a tournament, want to join?"

"Sure," I responded as I took a seat. Lisa eyed me up and down.

"How drunk are you?" She asked.

"I can still walk, so not very much?" I responded with slurred words.

She rolled her eyes, "Yeah, okay. Well, easy win for me then," she said, laughing. Lisa was not a drinker; she just liked to socialize.

Halfway through our game, Stacy and Brittany walked by, arm in arm. They saw me and immediately burst out laughing. I need another drink, I thought as I tried to ignore them. They went into the bathroom, still laughing. I lost that round and handed the controller to another competitor. I moved to the back of the room, away from the door. The bathroom door opened and I heard Stacy say, "She's no longer in there, maybe she went home, I hope. No one likes her anyway; she was only invited because we wanted to make sure she saw you with Christian." Brittany said, "Or maybe she came to be with Christian. If she did, I will kick her ass." Stacy laughed, "That would be awesome!"

*Great, add that to the list of people who want to beat me up.*

## CHAPTER 10

I sit at my desk, staring at the stack of papers that sit there, waiting for me. They need to be graded, but my mind is elsewhere. As a professor at the University of Colorado, my workload is insane.

After getting my Ph.D. in Psychology, I started my own practice on the outskirts of Boulder. I started teaching a few classes for the university after I graduated top of my class. I love teaching, but my heart is here at my office where I can help others. I take almost anyone but my focus is on children aged two years to eighteen. Kids who, like me, have had a shitty upbringing.

Todd, my therapist (ironic, I know), is who encouraged me to focus on this path, giving these children the help I needed but did not get. My phone rings and Bane, who is sitting at my feet, barks. "Hello, Dr. Anna Harding's office." I try to sound cheery but I doubt it fools anyone.

Silence. "Hello?" I repeat. Click. I stare at the phone. *That is weird.* I look at the clock. Seven p.m. *Shit.* I never intended to stay this late and the papers are still not graded. I call Rafe, "Hey babe, sorry, I am still at the office. I will be heading home soon." I say in a rush and Rafe laughs.

"Pizza for dinner then?" He says.

"I will pick some up. I love you," I say.

"Love you more." He says back. I smile. We hang up and I grab my keys and purse. As I grab Bane's leash, the office phone rings and I decide to let the answering machine get it. I need to get home to my husband and kids.

I get home at quarter to eight and the girls come barreling out of the house. "Pizza!" They squeal in unison. Dee takes the food and bolts for the house.

"Hey, Jessie, how is my favorite three-year-old?" I ask as I pick her up for a hug.

She squeezes my neck, "I was worried about you, mama!"

## PIECE BY PIECE

As I let Bane out of the jeep, I ask, "You were? Why, baby girl?"

I am still holding her and she squeezes my neck again, "I thought you and Bane were hurt by the bad man, mama."

I walk up the stairs of our deck to our back door, still carrying Jessie, "What bad man?"

She looks into my eyes, so full of worry, "The one who left a message on our phone saying he found you." I stop. *Don't react, don't let her see the worry and fear I am feeling.*

"I am right here, baby girl. No bad man got me or Bane, okay?" I say, hoping my voice is steady.

"Okay, mama. Can we have pizza now?"

I laugh and tickle her, "Yes baby, we can have pizza."

We walk inside and Rafe is standing in the kitchen with his back to the sink, arms crossed. Dee has already taken off with her pizza to the living room so I make Jessie a plate and send her to her sister. I turn to Rafe, "Why didn't you tell me when I called earlier, Rafe?" I said, trying to keep my voice calm.

"I did not know about it until after we hung up. Dee got home before me and heard it, then she played it for me."

*Fuck.* I run my hands through my hair. "I tried to call the office but got no answer so I thought you probably already left. Decided it would be best to wait till you got home," he finished.

"Someone called the office, but when I answered, no one said anything. When I said hello again, they hung up," as I tell Rafe this, it hits me. If he has my work and home numbers, then he knows where I live and probably more. I look around the kitchen in a panic.

"Anna, I already secured the house, security systems show nothing out of the ordinary." He says this to reassure me, but it doesn't. Rafe continues, "I think the girls should go to Mom and Dad's for a bit."

I nod in agreement. Rafe's dad is an ex-marine and his house is more safe than anywhere else I know. His security system and weapon room are enough to make the president's crew jealous.

"Dee can do her schoolwork online and you know Mom will make sure she does it," He says and I just nod, focusing my eyes on the pizza box.

"Anna?" He asks.

"Hmm?" I mumble.

"Anna, look at me."

I look at Rafe. His eyes show nothing. "When should we take them, Rafe?" I ask.

He sighs, "Dad is on his way now."

I nod again and say, "I will go pack their bags." Now, it is Rafe's turn to nod.

"We need to talk when they leave," Rafe says as he leaves the kitchen.

Thirty minutes later, Dee and Jessie are packed and in the car with Rafe's dad. "They will be safe with me, you know that, right, Anna?" Leland, Rafe's dad, says.

"I know, Dad, thank you." He nods, looking just like Rafe.

"You should come too, both of you," he says through the car window.

"I have to settle this for good, Dad. I can handle this. End this." He nods again, looking out his windshield.

## PIECE BY PIECE

"You know how much Rafe loves you, don't you?"

"Yes, I know," I respond quietly.

"He will die for you and these girls, but he will also kill for you. You mean everything to him," he says. I follow his gaze to Rafe who is standing in our doorway.

"Same, Dad, same." He pats my hand that is on his car door. "

Just make sure it is the second and not the first, okay?" I look him dead in the eyes.

"It will be, Dad."

He smiles, "Heart of a marine you got, kid." He starts the car and begins to back out then stops the car again, saying, "I love you, girl, and I am proud of you."

I am shocked as I watch him leave. "I love you too, Dad." I blow kisses to my girls till the tail lights fade. I walk back inside and lock the door. Rafe is already in the house somewhere. I double-check the security system. Bane is snoring by the back door so I leave him there. I take a long, hot shower, standing under the showerhead, trying to talk myself down from all the thoughts in my head. I dry off, brush my teeth, and grab my medication. Bupropion XL 300 mg and 75 mg; without it, I am a train wreck. I also take a sleep aid; insomnia is a bitch and she loves to have her nightmare friends take over if I do sleep. I swallow the pills and stare into the mirror. I don't recognize the woman looking back at me. The girl who once stared back is gone. I hurt for her; she never knew innocence, stability, trust, or love. The woman who has taken her place is haunted, but tough, strong, opinionated. The woman staring back took over, shielding the girl who once was, tucking her away in a safe place, never to be hurt again.

I walk into the bedroom and see Rafe lying on the bed, playing on his phone. He looks up and sees me, looking me dead in the eyes. I see so much in his eyes, possession, hunger, love, passion, and a promise. I shiver; I love that look in his eyes.

"Come here," he says in his deep voice. *Fuck, I love his voice.* My family used to joke that whatever man God had planned for me better be one tough son of a bitch, because I am untamable. I am stubborn and dominant. I submitted once in my life and it almost killed me in more ways than one.

Then there was Rafe. We met ten years ago through mutual friends. At first, I was just physically attracted, as that was all I could give at that time. Tall, lean, and quiet, Rafe had the body of a man who worked out by doing hours of manual labor, not at the gym. His quiet demeanor screamed dominance. He was a man who knew what he wanted, who knew who he was and didn't give a shit what others thought. What really got me were his eyes. He didn't even have to speak, not that he did much anyway. I knew what he wanted by the way he looked at me. It was like I could not fight it, I had to and wanted to submit to him.

Our relationship was very physical at first like we were teenagers again. For a man eight years older than me, I thought my drive was going to be too much for him. I was wrong.

"I said, come here, Anna," he repeated, breaking me from my trance. I went to him and climbed into bed next to him, his body like a full heat blanket around me.

"We need to talk," he says quietly. I close my eyes, not wanting to.

"Okay," is all I can say.

He sighs, "How do we handle this, Anna?"

"I don't know, Rafe."

"Should we call the cops?"

I laugh at that. I have the utmost respect for the police and military, but in my experience, cops do not have the power people think they do. "There is nothing they can do. The restraining order means nothing anymore, he was supposed to be locked up for life. Until he does something significant and I can prove it, they will just take a statement and say their hands are tied. I will handle it."

Rafe sighs again, "Quit saying *I*, Anna, it is *we,* okay? You are not alone, you will never be alone again, do you understand me?"

A tear slips down my face, "Yes, Rafe." He sits up on his side to face me. He wipes the tears away, "Don't cry, there is no reason to be scared. I won't let anything happen to you." I look up at him, lying flat on my back. The love I have for this man is like nothing I have ever felt before.

"I am not scared, Rafe. Not in the way you think. I am angry. Livid. That is what scares me, what I am capable of. Why was I not notified of his release? It's not like I disappeared, I am not hiding, they could have contacted me."

"I can't answer that, baby. All I know is he is out and he knows where you are and is now fucking with you, which means he is fucking with me and our girls. You know him better than I do, so tell me how you want to handle this."

I take a deep breath and release it before I answer. "This time, Rafe, there is only one way out of this." I look at him to gauge his reaction. His face gives nothing away.

"Well, I pray that it won't come to that, but if it does, I pray god protects us." He is right, we need to pray. I nod.

He leans in and kisses me. His mouth becomes more demanding and I submit. He tastes so good. His tongue finds mine and I let out a soft moan. His hands find my shirt and pull it up over my head. In nothing but panties, I am suddenly very insecure and shy. "Don't," he says, "do not try to cover yourself from me. You are gorgeous in every way." His mouth finds my neck, my weakness, and he trails his tongue to my ear. Chills cover my body even though he makes me feel like I am on fire. He rolls on top of me, his weight pinning me down. I love it, and I love him.

# CHAPTER 11

*Then*

Life of a high school girl is brutal and anyone who says differently is lying to you and themselves. I threw myself into any sport or activity I could to stay out of my house as much as possible. It was in track and field where I met a senior named Kevin. Again, small town, so his parents were friends with my mom and Bud. Kevin is super sweet and cute. We hit it off and he ended up asking me out to the school's Valentine's Day dance. I told him I would ask my mom but it should be okay. I was kind of excited to go with him. I preferred to go with Christian but I thought I could move on since he had. Or at least make it look like I have.

I got home from practice that night and bolted upstairs to find my mom. I end up finding Bud. *Fucking great.* "What's the hurry, Anna?" Bud asked, his eyes not leaving the television which had some sporting event on. We all learned quickly not to interrupt Bud when he was watching sports.

"Um, nothing, just looking for my mom," I said as I turned back to the stairs to leave the room.

"She is not home yet, you want to ask me something?" He replied as he glanced from the T.V. to me.

"No, why?" I mumbled because of what he said and how he said it confused me.

"You don't want to ask me if you can go to that dance with Kevin?" He asked, his tone was calm and not mean at all. *Weird. How in the hell did he find out already?*

As if reading my mind, Bud said, "Jack told me. Apparently, someone overheard him ask you and well, you know how fast news travels in this shit-hole town." *Well, he isn't wrong there.*

I nodded, "So much for me being able to ask y'all, huh?" He nodded; he hated this town but it was where his job was so he dealt with it.

I flopped down on the couch and sighed. He sighed as well, "So, do you want to go to this dance?" He sounded genuinely curious.

"I planned to go with Alex and meet Lisa there anyway, so yeah, I want to go." I responded.

Bud snorted. "I would rather you go with Kevin than Alex." Bud hated Alex, which is the reason I loved her even more.

"So, can I go with Kevin?" I asked, nervous about how calm he was being, considering how he was about Christian.

"You can go, but he has to meet you there, you know the rules, no actual dates till you are sixteen."

I nodded. "Fair. Does Jack have to take me?" I asked, thinking of backing out of the whole thing if he did.

Bud laughed, "No, your mom can drop you off. If she doesn't know by now, I will let you tell her. I also told Jack to keep his mouth shut."

"Okay, thank you," I responded in shock that we actually had a civil conversation.

## PIECE BY PIECE

It was the night of the dance and I was nervous. Why? The dress my mom helped me pick out was gorgeous and not something I would normally wear. Red, form-fitting, with matching heels. I hated the heels, but my mom said boots were not flattering my dress. My long brown hair was curled and fell down my back. I did not recognize myself. So different from the boots, jeans, and hoodies I normally wore. I headed upstairs to where the whole "family" was waiting.

Mom burst into tears, "My baby! You look so grown up!"

"Holy shit! You're a girl?" Jack blurted out.

Bud smacked him upside his head, "Jack, watch your mouth." He then looked at me, "Beautiful, kid. You know how much I love your hair." I knew that, and it sickened me.

"Thanks, everyone. And Jack, even while looking like this, I can still kick your ass."

Bud laughed at that, "Of that, I have no doubt." Jack turned red.

Jo-jo tapped my leg and said, "Anna, you look like a princess!" I picked her up and gave her a hug, "*You're* the princess, my jo-jo."

PIECE BY PIECE

"We should go," my mom said.

We got to the school and Kevin was waiting for me outside. He opened my door, waving to my mom. He took my hand to help me out of the car. I waved to my mom and we walked to the door.

"You look unbelievably gorgeous, Anna," Kevin said as we headed to the gym.

"Thank you," I replied shyly.

"I mean it, you're stunning," he said as he put his hand at the small of my back, leading me in.

The music was blaring and the gym was packed full of students already. Red and pink balloons, streamers, and tables filled the gym. The DJ was at the far end of the gym with room for dancing. There were already some kids dancing, and many were standing with friends along the dance space of the gym. Alex and Lisa rushed over and we gushed over each other's dresses. We took a seat at a table close to the DJ. Kevin leaned in since it was so hard to hear over the music. "I am going to go say hi to the guys and grab a drink, do you want one?" he asked. I nodded and mouthed "thank you." He gave me a big grin before he headed off. The "Cupid Shuffle" came on and all three of us jumped up to go dance. I kicked off my heels first, knowing I would break an ankle if I didn't. I got lost in the song, laughing with Alex and Lisa. The song ended and I saw Kevin waiting at the table with our drinks.

"Sorry, I love that song," I said to him as I sat down and slammed the water down he got for me.

"Don't be, I want you to have a good time and I did love watching you dance." He grinned at me and I shyly smiled in response. "All My Life" by K-Ci and JoJo came on. "Do you want to dance with me?" Kevin asked.

"Yes," I stammered. Other than with Christian, in his room, I had never danced with anyone before. He took my hand, leading me to the dance floor. His hands found my waist as I wrapped my arms around his neck. He pulled me closer and whispered in my ear, "Is this okay?" I nodded at him and gave him another shy smile.

As we danced, a few of our friends came by, nudging us and making kissy faces. I rolled my eyes and looked over Kevin's shoulder. My eyes locked with Christian. *Fuck, he's here.* He looked pissed. I turned my attention back to Kevin, trying hard not to look back. "You okay?" Kevin asked me.

## PIECE BY PIECE

"Yeah, I'm fine," I replied.

"Are you sure? You look upset, did I-" I cut him off.

"No, no, Kevin, you're great, seriously, I am good." I told him with a smile that I hoped would reassure him and hide my pain. It worked. The song ended and we went back to our table. For not being much of a drinker, I could use one right now. We danced some more through the night, laughing with our friends. I didn't see Christian again that night and I started to wonder if I imagined him being there. Then "Amazed" by Lonestar came on. *Our song.*

Kevin asked me to dance but I declined, "I need to sit this one out, need more water, and rest a bit." My attempt to reassure him worked. The song ended, thank God. He went to get us water and I thanked him. Alex and Lisa were dancing with a couple of guys from our class so I was alone at the table. I saw Christian again, and my heart stopped. He was on the dance floor with Brittany. They were dancing to our song, it seemed like! She was in a red dress with her brown hair curled and hanging down, just like me. I felt like I was going to throw up. He locked eyes with me, his expression giving nothing away. I didn't want to react but I could feel the panic attack hitting me with full force. The tears gathered in my eyes. I needed to get out of there immediately. That was our fucking song, that asshole! I got up and headed for the door, gasping for air. The tears fell and I cursed myself for being so weak and stupid.

"Anna?" I heard Kevin calling my name from behind me. Shit.

I quickly wiped the tears and turned to him, "Hey, um, sorry it was so hot in there. I needed air, I got sweaty. Gross, I know." I smiled to try and show that I was fine.

He cocked his head, "So hot you ran?" I nodded, I had no excuse for that.

"Anna, was it Christian? Did he say or do something to upset you?" He asked quietly.

I let out a nervous laugh, "No, Kevin, he didn't. I could care less that he is here."

"Then why are you crying?" He asked, voice full of concern. We sat down on the bench outside the school, and he took my hand. "You can talk to me, Anna, okay?" I just nodded at him. I couldn't tell him the truth, I couldn't tell anyone.

"Kevin, do you mind if we just stay here for a bit, please?" I asked him.

He nodded, "Of course, we can, can I ask you something though?"

"Sure," I said as I turned to face him.

"Would you be interested at all in being my girlfriend?"

His question catches me off guard, "Really? Me? Why?" I was seriously confused and still worked up over seeing Christian with that bitch.

He sighed, "Well, you're smart, funny, gorgeous and, I don't know, something about you just pulls me in, I can't explain it."

I took in his words, debating on whether I believed him or not. "Okay," I said to him, smiling. Christian moved on with some tramp who didn't know her ass from a hole in the ground, so why couldn't I with a genuine guy?

"Okay?" He asked.

I smiled wide at him, saying "Okay, Kevin, I will be your girlfriend if you are fine with me being a freshman and your friends giving you shit about it." He laughed and his grin was so big.

"I don't care if you're a freshman, I can handle my friends. Can I kiss you now? Been waiting all night."

"Yes, you can, since you have been so deprived all night," I said with a chuckle. He kissed me and it was really good. I had to push away the voice in my head telling me that it was not Christian.

*Now*

Rafe and I agree that we need to go about our lives like nothing is wrong and the girls are having their own little vacation with their grandma and grandpa. If Jack is fucking with me and watching me, I want him to see I am not scared or on edge, that he has no effect on me other than annoying me.

Bane and I take to the trail for our run. I need this. This is how I handle my stress, fears, hurt, and anger. Besides angrily cleaning the house, this is how I deal with my emotions. I run. It is definitely better than how I used to handle it all.

Memories flood my mind as I keep my pace. Jo-jo was one and a half years old, she was crying and making Bud mad. I couldn't get her to calm down. My mom was at work. Bud picked her up by the front of her onesie, shaking her and telling her to "shut the fuck up!" I couldn't stop him as he slammed her down onto the couch, her screaming getting worse. I ran into his office with a lighter. If I could set his chair on fire, the fire department and cops would come and I could tell them. Anything to take the attention off Josie.

I pick up my pace as another memory hits. All four of us kids, on our hands and knees, picking the dandelions in the front yard, one at a time. If we spoke to anyone, each other or our friends who came by, we got the belt. I run faster, my mind filled with Bud and then Jack's insults. Bud's slaps, punches, and hair pulling. "You will never amount to shit! You will end up being some trailer trash whore whose husband beats you! You'll have ten kids all with different dads!" I hear their voices over and over. My lungs burn, but I welcome the pain. I run deeper into the wood trail behind our house, Bane keeping pace and never leaving my side. He gets me. The screams of my siblings and my mom all ring in my ears. The tears start to fall. I reach the top of the cliffs along the trail and stop. I am gasping for air, bawling my eyes out, and overcome with such anger that I can feel and see the darkness swallowing me, blinding me. *No!* "Fuck you!" I scream loudly, "I am not scared of you! Either of you! Do you hear me, Jack? You fucking coward!" The cliff echoes my words, Bane stares at me like I have lost my mind.

I close my eyes and pray, "God, I know no fear because you are with me. Keep me strong. How will I know I am safe?" An image of Rafe, smiling at me, fills my mind. I open my eyes and see Bane, who is rubbing against me to comfort me. God did not answer me outright with words, of course, but the feeling of knowing I am safe washes over me. The darkness goes away, I swear I can see it hidden in the trees around me. The fear, anger, and hurt all disappear. I look at the sky and grin. "I hear you, God. You gave me Rafe and Bane, and I have you!" Bane barks. I laugh and give him a hug. "I love you, boy. Let's go home." We head back to the house.

*Then*

Things with Kevin were good, he was a good guy. My mom and Bud approved, so there was that. I liked him a lot, but he wasn't Christian. I did not feel the safety, the love, the need, the pull with Kevin like I did with Christian. There was attraction, obviously, but not like I had with Christian. I started to think that no one will compare or come close to him.

After a rough practice, I got home, wanting nothing more than to take a shower and go to bed. "Dinner is ready!" I heard my mom yell; I wasn't even hungry. Dinner was not negotiable in our house. We had to eat "as a family" and no one was allowed to start till everyone had their food. Bud was always served first, always. Then we prayed before we ate, I didn't know why, it's not like God gave a shit anyway, especially about me.

I got to the table and once we began eating, Bud did his usual "what-happened-at-school" bonding session. *Fucking gag me.* When it got to my turn, I ran through my same old speech.

"How are things with you and Kevin?" My mom asked me.

"Good," was all I replied with.

"You have not fucked it up yet, uh?" Bud asked.

"Apparently not, Bud," I answer, already feeling myself getting tense and defensive, picking at my food.

"Do not get smart with me, girl, it was just a question," his tone laced with irritation. "You know, Anna, if you wore your hair down more, you would look way better. Guys, good guys, would pay more attention," Bud said. *What the actual fuck?* That made no sense to me. I made a "that's bullshit" face and told him,

"I do not need attention." *I want this conversation over.* He chuckled dismissively. "Of course, you do. You love attention of any kind, it surprises me that you do not use the one good thing God gave you for it. Your hair," he said, taking another bite

# PIECE BY PIECE

of food. I nodded, whatever it took to get him to shut the fuck up. Then, an idea hit me.

"Speaking of my hair," I said, "Mom, it needs a trim. Maybe then I would wear it down more if the ends did not look like crap."

Bud smiled creepily, "See, it is so much better if you just do as I say."

"I will make the appointment tomorrow," my mom says.

"Thanks." I responded. I was over everybody's bullshit, it was time to really start looking out for myself. And Jojo, of course.

## CHAPTER 12

*Then*

My hair appointment was only a week away and I could not wait! After practice, Kevin asked to talk to me. *Great, now what?*

"Hey, so I have been doing some thinking and with me graduating this year, I think it would be best if we split up. I will be leaving and you still have three years left, it is not fair to either of us," he stated. *Getting dumped sucks.*

"Okay," is all I could say.

"Okay? That's it? You're not mad?" He asked me, genuinely confused.

I smiled at him. "I cannot make you stay with me, Kevin, and your reasons make sense. Plus, you've already made the decision for us, for me." Just like everyone else in my life, I thought to myself.

"If I go to college and you are what I think about before I go to bed and when I wake up, I will come back for you," he said.

"Okay," I replied. *Yeah right is more like it.* It didn't surprise me, no guy ever wanted me. Not even my own father, my stepdad, friends, boyfriends, or even God Himself. I was just a plain object so why would that be any different? I walked away.

I got to the house and went straight to the shower to bawl my eyes out. I felt worthless, unwanted, unprotected. After I got dressed, I headed upstairs to eat. Jack was up there and grinned at me. *Creepy fuck.*

"I heard you got dumped! Once a guy gets what he wants from you, you get discarded," he said in his arrogant and cynical voice, "How does it feel to be trash?"

With no emotion, I replied, "At least I was wanted at all, Jack," I pursed my lips and make a sad face, "You, on the other hand, are complete shit. No one wants that," I said in a voice that sounded like I was having pity on him.

All of a sudden, he punched me in the gut, hard. "Fuck you, cunt!" I grinned, trying to hide the pain from his punch.

"I would rather not, dumbass. That's gross." He shoved me and I saw black. I don't remember what or how, but when I could see again, my mom was pulling me off Jack and he was crying, curled in a ball on the floor.

"Anna! What the hell!" My mom yelled at me.

"He hit me first!" I yelled back.

"No, I did not! You're lying, you crazy psycho!" Jack cried, getting up, "She gets dumped and then takes it out on me!"

"Is that true?" My mom asked.

I rolled my eyes and said, "It's true I got dumped, but I didn't hit him first! It was self-defense after he punched me in the stomach!"

Jack wiped the blood off his mouth and showed it to my mom. "Look! She made me bleed!"

I grinned, "Pussy!"

"That is enough!" Mom cut in. "Jack, go get cleaned up. Anna, what happened with Kevin?"

I spread my arms out and shrugged, "Does it matter?"

"Are you okay?" She asked. "I'm perfectly fine, Mom." I turned to go back down to my room and saw Bud standing in the entryway. *Great.* He said nothing and I could not tell what his expression meant. I ignored him and went to bed.

The next morning, my mom took me to town for my hair appointment. "I am going to go run errands while you get your hair done," she said as she pulled to the curb.

"If I pay for it, can I get highlights?" I asked her.

She sighed, "I don't know, Anna. We should discuss it with Bud first, don't you think?" She asked me. No, we should not, I thought.

"Mom, I just got dumped, got into it with Jack, and I am supposed to go to my dad's for two weeks if he remembers. I need to do something for myself, please."

She sighed again and said, "Okay, I get it. You can get highlights." I smiled, thanked her, and headed into the salon.

# PIECE BY PIECE

Two hours later, I walked out of the salon to my mom's car. I climbed in and she hadn't looked at me yet.

"It will be fine, Bud, she's almost 15 years old and with her dad more than likely to pull some shit, she needed to do that for herself, it won't be as bad as you..." She looked at me and her eyes went huge, "Um, Bud, let me call you back." She hung up and stared at me. "Anna! What the hell have you done? Oh god, your hair! Bud is going to flip! We are both dead! You said highlights!" She said frantically.

I looked in the visor mirror at my new mid-neck-length blonde hair. I loved it. "I decided I needed a big change," I said casually.

"What in the fuck were you thinking!" She was getting mad.

"I was thinking that I love it," I responded with a shrug of my shoulders.

She huffed. "Bud is going to kill us both!" I smirked, mentally daring him to try.

The ride to the house was quiet. Not even music was on. We pulled up and Josie and Rhea came running out of the house,

"Oh, Anna! Your hair! What happened?" Rhea asked, practically crying.

"I needed a change," I replied as I picked up Jojo.

"I like it, Anna!" Josie beamed at me.

"Thanks, Jojo," I told her, giving her a kiss on the cheek.

Rhea ran ahead of me to the door, saying, "Dad is going to flip, I am going to go hide in my room." I saw Jack in the front window of the living room. He ran his thumb across his neck, a clear sign that I was fucked.

I walked inside, setting Josie down. "Want to play hide and seek?" I asked her, looking her dead in the eyes.

"Yes, I will hide first," Josie responded quietly.

I smiled. "I will find you," and she took off. Even my mom, a coward, went to her and Bud's room and shut the door. *So much for support.*

Bud was in the kitchen, back against the counter, arms folded over his chest. The look on his face told me I better not say a word. I was so tired of being afraid of him though. "Hey Bud! What's up?" I said cheerfully, not a hint of fear in my voice.

His face was beet red and his teeth gritted together, snarling at me. I kept going, "You okay, Bud? You look sick," I said as I went over to the fridge.

Finally, he said through clenched teeth, "What the fuck did you do?" He practically had smoke coming out of his ears. *Good, hope the bastard's head explodes.*

"Oh, I cut my hair and colored it, obviously. Don't you like it? I love it!" I took a sip of the water I grabbed from the fridge. I could see Jack in the living room, shock on his face, looking between Bud and me.

Bud said from behind me, "And you thought I would be okay with this?" I sighed and turned around, looking him dead in his eyes.

"Honestly Bud, I didn't even take what you would think into consideration. I took what *I* would think into consideration and *I* love it." I said, never looking away from him or even blinking.

"So, you are an adult now? Making your own decisions?" He taunted me, his teeth still clenched.

"No, I never said I was. The decision on what to do to my body is mine, no one owns it but me, including my hair," I said as I crossed my arms over my chest to match his demeanor.

In less than two strides, he was across the kitchen with his fist tangled in my now short blonde hair. He jerked my head back and his face was in mine, practically touching noses. I didn't react; I had been conditioned not to since I was four years old. A reaction was just what he wanted. The pain was real, his nasty breath was real, and I cringed at it.

He was almost spitting in my face, "That is where you are wrong, little girl. I own you! As long as you live in my house and eat my food, I own you and now you have fucked up!"

I grinned at him, letting him see that he had no power over me and I had no fear of him, saying, "You mean the food and house that my dad's child support payments help with? Isn't that what it is for? Or did I fuck up there too?"

He pulled my hair hard, making it feel like it was getting ripped from my scalp. "Your daddy doesn't even want you, you little bitch! Not that I blame him for that, but the only reason he pays is because the court says he does and the military makes him. It's not because he wants to provide for you!" He spat and shoved me back. "*I* provide for you. I am more of a dad than he will ever be, you ungrateful brat!"

I burst out laughing, hysterically, and Jack's mouth dropped in disbelief. "You find that funny?" Bud asked, way too calmly. He was changing tactics to try to throw me off.

I calmed down and gave him the most smartass grin I could. "Yes Bud, I do find it funny. You are not my dad and you never will be. You are an asshole who gets off on beating children! My mom might be scared of you, Jack, Rhea, and Josie, too," My voice was raising, but I continued, "but not me. You don't scare me at all!"

The first backhand came to the left side of my face. The second connected with my mouth and I tasted blood. White hot pain shot through my face. Everything went black and I remember nothing after that second hit. When I came to, I was on the couch and my mom was standing between me and Bud, begging me to stop as he took his belt off.

I was pretty sure he was going to kill me. "You mouthy, ungrateful little bitch! You want to swing at me again? You are done, fucking done!" He screamed at me. The phone rang and everyone stopped. Bud grabbed it and answered without looking at the caller ID.

"What!" He yelled into the phone. Then, he locked eyes with me and said, "Yeah, hold on." He handed me the phone. "Saved by the bell, little girl, it's *daddy*," he dragged the last word out sarcastically.

I took the phone and my mom whispered, "Not a word, Anna!"

"Hello, daddy!" I said, trying to keep my voice calm. "Hey, Anna Banana!" my dad's voice sang. I really hated when he called me that. "How are things? You okay? I can tell Bud loves you. Good man!" He laughed as he said it.

"I'm fine, Dad, just rough-housing with the other kids." I had gotten really good at lying and hiding all the bullshit.

"Cool! You are dominating, of course?" He said. He wanted a boy but got me instead, so of course, he treated me like I was a boy.

"Of course, whooping some butt!" I replied and Bud snorted.

# PIECE BY PIECE

"So, Anna, I know I am supposed to come get you soon, but um, I can't do it this time, baby girl." Shocker, I think to myself, "I promise that you can come this summer, okay?" I rolled my eyes.

"Yeah, Dad, no big deal, I get it." That was another lie I had been getting good at. We talked a few more minutes before we hung up.

"Let me guess," Bud started sarcastically. "Daddy isn't coming?" I handed him back the phone with no reaction and headed down the stairs to my room. I could hear him and my mom begin to argue.

I waited a few minutes in my room before I went to look for Jojo. I had taught her to hide and not make a sound until I was the one who found her. I made sure no one was around or spying, like Jack. I opened the door to her hiding spot. "Come out now, Jojo, it's okay," I told her calmly as I helped her out of the spot we came up with that no one would guess.

"Are you okay, Anna?" She asked me as her little hands touched the bruise already forming on my cheek. I smiled at her. "I am good, Jojo, I promise," I said in an attempt to reassure her.

# PIECE BY PIECE

"You are the toughest person I know, Anna," she told me as she hugged my neck. I had to be, for her.

## CHAPTER 13

I get to my office at about 9 a.m. My first appointment isn't until 10:30, so I start grading papers. My secretary, Sandra, walks in with a small bouquet of flowers. They are not from Rafe; he doesn't do flowers.

"Mine?" I ask, confused.

"Yup, a man dropped them off a few minutes ago," she says to me. Maybe Rafe is trying to make me feel better, but this is not his normal way of doing that. Sandra leaves my office and I grab the card stuck in the middle and open it. Right away, I know whose handwriting it is. My hands start to shake as I read what he wrote. "You can scream in the woods all you want, you can say you're not scared, but we both know you are. He cannot save you, no one can."

# PIECE BY PIECE

There is no signature. *Damn it.* I walk out of my office towards Sandra at the front desk. "Who brought the flowers to you, Sandra?" I ask, trying to keep my voice as even as I can.

She looks at me, puzzled. "I'm not sure, I have never seen him before, I just assumed he was from the flower shop doing deliveries."

I let out a long, slow breath. "Can you describe him for me, please?"

"Uh, yeah, he was about six foot tall and had beady, dark eyes. He had a hat on and seemed nervous to talk to me, but his laugh was obnoxious. Why? Something wrong?" She asks me with clear concern on her face.

"Oh no, I was just curious. Can you call and reschedule all my appointments today? I am so behind on my grading and it will take me all day to get caught up," I tell her as I start to head back to my office.

"Yeah, no problem," she answers, eyeing me suspiciously.

I go back to my office and shut the door. I lean my back against it, trying to calm down. Bane whines at me and I crouch down to his level to pet him and reassure him that I am fine.

Fighting the panic attack I feel coming on, I go to my desk. I pull up the security footage from that morning to see if it can show me who the man was. I find it and Sandra was right, not that I doubted her. He had a hat on and he kept his face away from the cameras. I would know that stance and walk anywhere; it was Jack. He was there for just a minute and then he was gone, which was enough time to drop the flowers off and leave. I put my head on my desk and fold my hands above them. "God, whatever your plan is with this, I trust you. I just need you to help calm me, help me think clearly and rationally." A vision of Rafe crosses my mind and I smile. Of course. Rafe is the rational one, the complete opposite of me; he evens me out.

I pick up the phone and call Rafe at work. "Hey baby," he answers on the second ring.

"Hey, have you got a minute to talk?" I ask, trying to hide the panic I feel.

"Yeah, what's up?" I begin to replay the whole morning to him, except for the part where God showed him as the answer to my prayer. I want to keep that between me and God only. He is silent for what seems like forever.

"Rafe?" I ask.

I hear him let out a long slow breath as he answers, "Do we call the cops now?" He suggests in a voice that is way too calm.

"There was no name on the card, his back was to the security cameras, so there is no evidence that it was him. I also doubt any florist would have security cameras that got him as well, he is too smart for that. He could have gotten them anywhere and paid with cash so there is no trail," I answer him.

"Motherfucker!" His snap makes me jump back, even if it is over the phone. "Do I need to come get you?" He asks.

"No, no, I'm okay, seriously Rafe," I say to reassure him.

"My phone is on loud, call me and I will be there. Keep Bane with you, okay?" He demands.

"Okay," is all I can say.

"Anna?" He asks, his voice softer now.

"Yeah, Rafe?"

"I love you, you hear me?" He almost sounds scared, but that is not possible. Rafe is not scared of anything, ever. I smile, even though he can't see me.

"I love you more, Rafe." We hang up and I try to get back to my grading.

*Then*

My track meet just so happened to be at the same school as the baseball team's, so that meant my track team rode the same bus with Christian's baseball team. My hair had shocked a lot of people, especially him. We did not speak much, but when he first saw me with my new hair, he looked disappointed. Of course, I could not tell him why I did it or I would have to explain it all and that was something I could not do. He sat at the back of the bus, and I sat more towards the front, but I could feel him watching me. Or maybe I imagined it, I couldn't bring myself to check. Luckily, the opposing school was not too far away, so when we got there, I got off the bus as fast as I could and took off for the track field.

The track meet ended about halfway through the ball game, so our team went to watch the rest of the baseball game to cheer the boys on. I saw Mrs. O'Rion in the stands and she smiled so big at me that the world got brighter, at least for me anyway. She gestured for me to sit by her on the bleachers and gave me a big hug when I got to her. The hug lasted longer than any hug I ever had before, especially from a parent, including my own. She then held me at arm's length and touched my hair. "I love it, Anna! Now you truly are my ray of sunshine!" My heart broke a little, I missed her so much. We sat down to watch the game and I could not tell Christian was not happy with me sitting next to his mom. I pretended not to notice him frowning at me.

"You know," Mrs. O'Rion said to me with a sideways glance, "Christian and Brittany broke up." She looked at me dead on.

"Oh, I didn't know, that sucks for them. I'm sorry," I responded, pretending that I couldn't care less. I hated lying to her, even like that, but she could never know the truth as well.

"She is not you, Anna," she said, touching my arm as a show of affection. *Ain't that the truth*, I think to myself.

I gave her a small laugh and said "I am one of a kind!" with a shrug.

Her face looked pained, "Is it true that the reason you broke up with my son is because you were not ready for the commitment of a relationship?"

## PIECE BY PIECE

That was the first time we had ever spoken about it. I kept telling myself not to cry. All I could do was nod and look out at the game. I couldn't look her in the eyes or she would have seen the truth.

"Anna, look at me, please," her voice broke my heart.

I looked at her, holding back the tears like I had taught myself to do. *"Crying gets you nowhere. No one feels sorry for you just because you cry!"* Bud's words echoed in my head. She eyed me suspiciously; I had a feeling she didn't believe me.

"You know you can talk to me, right? About anything, I won't judge you or make you feel stupid." I nodded again, because I had no words for her. "There is more to it, isn't there?" She pushed. She could read me like a book, better than my own mother. "Nothing can be done about it, momma O," I said. She nodded. I knew my answer hurt her and it killed me. She turned back to the game. "You still love him, don't you? I can tell." Once again, all I could do was nod. I always will, for the rest of my life, I think to myself.

The next week at school, I was at my locker, getting ready to head to practice as all the other students were getting ready to go home. "Hey, Anna." My heart and body froze. *Christian.*

That was the first time in months he had acknowledged me at all. I turned to face him, hoping I looked bored already, even if I was freaking out inside. "Hey Christian, what's up?" I responded like he was just a friend and not the guy who owned my heart. He smiled. *Damn him.* "Not hey Chris?" He said. I wrinkled my nose at him and replied, "Nah, doesn't sound right." He laughed. "Well, hearing it from you doesn't sound right." I just smiled back. I missed him so bad it physically hurt. "So, what's up, Christian?"

He sighed. "Nothing really, just thought I should say hi and ask why you did that to your hair," he said as he nodded to my hair. I shut my locker and started walking to the gym.

I stopped at the exact spot we met and turned to face him since he followed me for an answer. "I needed a change," I answered.

He nodded and asked, "Is that your way of making a statement that you are moving on?"

I took a deep breath. No matter what I said, it would be a lie. He could never know the truth. I answered, "In a way, yes."

He looks at me with his beautiful eyes and says, "From me." It was a statement, not a question.

PIECE BY PIECE

I tilted my head at him a little, "Not exactly, no."

A movement behind Christian caught my attention. Jack. He was watching us with a smug look on his face. *Fuck, I'm dead.* Christian followed my gaze, then looked back at me, seemingly unbothered by Jack. "Then what exactly is it, Anna?"

I struggled with my words, anxiety settling in. "Uh, nothing, I can't tell you, I mean, I don't know. Look, Christian, I've got to go."

He looked pissed. "Okay." I turned and booked it to the locker room.

After practice, I headed home, not knowing what to expect. Another backhand probably. I walked in like it was just another normal day.

"Hey, Anna! Wash up, supper is almost ready!" My mom called down the stairs. I did what she asked and met everyone at the table. We began to eat. Halfway through the meal, Bud looked at me and said, "So Anna, how was school?" I could tell by his tone what he was hinting at.

"Um fine, same old stuff," I answered, not looking away from my food.

He continued, "And practice?" He had never asked me that before. I looked at him and I could see it on his face that he knew. *Don't react.*

"Good, lots of gassers," I said, referring to the coach's favorite drill of starting at the end zone of the football field and running by 10 yards and back till it was end zone to end zone. It was brutal.

"Nothing else happened?" He looked at me with accusing eyes. I looked at him, faking confusion,

"Like what?"

"You tell me," he said in a controlled voice. I set my fork down and let out a breath.

"Well, Bud, I don't know what you are talking about, so you tell me," I said, point blank.

"Watch your tone, girl," he warned me.

"I'm just saying I don't know what you're talking about," I replied as innocently as I could.

"Did you talk to Christian today?" He asked, expecting me to lie. I sighed again.

"In passing. I was headed to practice and he asked me why I did this to my hair," I responded, pointing to my hair.

He nodded. "That is not what I was told."

I snapped my gaze to Jack. "Your little minion here," I said, pointing to Jack, "did not hear the full conversation, and for the record, Jack, you're really creepy for spying on me like that, you pervert. Congratulations on nailing the stalker vibe."

Bud was on his feet, his chair hitting the wall. "Shut the fuck up! You were told not to talk to that boy!" He yelled at me. Rhea and Jojo stopped eating and looked terrified, which set me off.

My mom interrupted. "Bud, honestly, this is a small town, small school, they are going to see each other in passing."

He turned his anger towards her. "Shut the fuck up! I didn't ask you!"

I stood up and said to him calmly, "Do not talk to my mom like that."

My mom looked at me, terrified. "Anna, don't!" She begged me. Someone had to stand up to that prick and I had been doing it since I was 4 years old, so why stop then?

# PIECE BY PIECE

"What did you say to me?" His fists balled up at his sides.

"I did not stutter, but if you need me to repeat it, fine. I said, do not talk to my mom like that!"

He rounded Jack's chair and grabbed my arm faster than I could react. I fell to the floor and he grabbed me by my shirt and jerked me back up. I made no sound; I wouldn't give him the satisfaction. He pinched the skin under my chin with his fat fingers. It hurt so bad but I still didn't react. My mom yelled for him to stop and he told her to shut up.

He turned back to me. "Do you think I am a dumbass?"

I said nothing because he wouldn't like my answer. He jerked me by his hold on my neck. "Answer me!"

I clenched my teeth and mentally prepared myself for what was to come. Behind him, Jack and Rhea are watching with huge eyes. Josie had her eyes squeezed shut and her hands over her ears. My mom was just standing there, her eyes pleading with me to give in. *Sorry, Mom, I'm not you.*

I looked him dead in the eyes, his grip not any looser. "Do you want the truth of what I think or do you want me to lie to you to make you feel better?"

He chuckled. "You got balls, girl, I'll give you that." He got as close to my face as he could and whispered, "You know what happens if you go back to him." He shoved me back, sitting in his chair again, and started eating like nothing happened.

# CHAPTER 14

*Now*

"He will fuck up, Rafe, he always does." I say as Rafe paces our kitchen.

"So until he does, we can't do anything? Even the police?" He retorts.

I sigh, "Unfortunately, none of us can do anything till he does."

Rafe stops, facing the sink, both hands gripping the rim of it. "So, you're telling me, your life is at risk again because of that piece of shit and we have to wait till he tries to kill you?"

I shrug. "Pretty much, but Rafe, he won't kill me."

He starts pacing again. "Fucking right he won't, I won't let him."

The phone rings then and Rafe answers it. "Hello?" He then looks at me, "Hold on." He hands me the phone. I take it as Rafe goes to the other side of the kitchen island.

I put the phone to my ear "Hello?" I ask nervously.

"Hey Anna!" I sigh in relief; it's my mom.

"Hey mom." I say. "How are things?" She asks. Either she has no clue or she does but wants me to bring it up. "Well, Mom, Jack is here."

I hear her intake of breath, "What!" She practically screams into the phone. "Let me finish, Mom, let me tell you everything before you flip shit."

I tell her about the phone calls, the flowers, and that there is no way to prove it is him right now. She lets out a breath. "You know what your dad and brother are going to say and do right?" I smile. Derek, a.k.a. my dad, and my step-brother, Jason, are super protective. My mom married Derek when I was an adult, but he has proven what a real dad should be. His son, Jason, has taught me what it means to rely on someone, to count on them in everything.

"Tell them that I've got it handled, Mom." She snorts.

"Yeah, they won't care, I bet you money as soon as Jason finds out he will be on the first flight there. Your dad too, I'm guessing." She is right.

"The girls are staying with Rafe's parents till this is handled." I say to reassure her, but really to reassure myself.

"That is a really good idea." She says, then it goes quiet. *Damn it.*

"What is it?" I ask her, feeling that I will not like what she is about to tell me.

"Josie, she is uh, she is blaming herself again." She tells me. *Fuck.* I let out a breath I was holding in, I feel I have been doing that a lot lately.

"I will call her, Mom." My mom starts sobbing. "Mom, stop it. It will be alright, okay?" I say to try and calm her down.

"I am such a horrible mom, Anna, or at least I was. Back then. I am so sorry." Do not cry, I tell myself.

"Mom, no you're not. He was abusive to you too, just not physically. We have discussed this already. I don't blame you. Josie and I turned out just fine, and that is because of you, not him." I say to reassure her.

She sniffles, "How did I get so lucky to get you as my daughter?"

I laugh, "God thought you needed extra stress in your life so you got me."

She laughs before going quiet again. "What are you going to do, Anna?" She finally asks me.

"What I have to mom, we both know that." I answer her.

"No matter what happens, you know I love you." She replies.

"I love you too, Mom." Then we hang up. Rafe and I look at each other and say nothing. There is nothing to say.

I walk out to the porch and light a cigarette before I call Josie. I am going to need it.

"Hey Anna." She answers on the first ring, her tone quiet and soft. She is scared.

## PIECE BY PIECE

"Hey my Jojo, what's up?" I say, trying to sound upbeat.

"Uh, um, nothing." She says in response.

I cut to the chase, "Jack is here, Josie."

Her tone suddenly becomes frantic. "I swear, Anna, I did not tell him! He asked but I told him no!"

I pinch the bridge of my nose, trying to get rid of the coming headache.

"Shhh, Jojo, just stop. I know you didn't tell him, honey, okay? This is all on him and I will handle this." I tell her to try and calm her down.

"You always handle it, Anna. Ever since I was born." She says between sniffles. "He has not called me in a while."

"You will let me know if he does, right Jojo?" I ask her.

"Of course, Anna." She says eagerly.

"Josie, seriously, none of this is your fault. You just call me if you need anything."

She laughs, "You can't take care of me forever, Anna. You have your own family!" She presses.

I make sure my tone is serious and stern. "First of all, you are my family too. Second, I will do what I want and what I want is for you to stay safe and healthy."

"You always do what you want, Anna, always have." I laugh now.

"Damn right, little one. I love you Jojo."

That night, I climb in bed early. I feel physically and emotionally drained. I know I will not sleep, but my bed is calling me. I waste my time scrolling through social media.

Rafe comes to bed about thirty minutes later. "Hey, I thought you would be asleep by now." He says to me.

"I doubt I will sleep till this is all over." I say honestly. He kisses my forehead.

"Let me take a quick shower, then we can talk." He says as he heads to our master bathroom. I go back to looking through my phone.

The house phone rings and I am immediately out of bed and on edge. Every part of my body became alert. I pick up the phone to check the caller ID. It reads "unavailable," and on the third ring, I pick it up. "Hello." I try to say as calmly as I can.

## PIECE BY PIECE

"Hey, mommy!" Jessie's voice fills the air. I instantly relax and want to cry.

"Hey, my girl! How is my sweet baby?" I reply.

"I miss you and daddy," she whines to me.

"I know, sweetheart, me too. But aren't you having fun with Grandma and Grandpa?"

"Yes, Grandpa is teaching us how to do missions!" *Of course he is*, I laugh to myself.

"Oh goodness! Missions, huh?"

"Yeah, he got us nerf guns and ammo and we sneak around the house learning um… um… Grandpa!" I hear her call out to her grandfather. "What am I learning again?" I hear her ask him. I can hear him chuckle in the back ground and say, "Tactical training and gun safety."

"Mom, we are learning batical trains and gun safely." I laugh. *Oh stay young and innocent.*

"Hey, brat! I want to talk to Mom too!" I hear Dee yell. I roll my eyes. Jessie snaps back, "I'm no brat! You're stupid!"

I cut off their argument, "Okay, okay, Jessie, let me talk to your sister."

Jessie lets out a big sigh. "Ugh fine! Bye Mommy, I love you!"

"I love you too, Jessie." I hear my mother-in-law telling Jessie to hand the phone to Dee nicely.

"Hey Mom." I hear Dee now.

"Hey Dee, how are you?" I ask her.

"I'm fine, how are you and dad?" She asks. She sounds just like me when I was her age.

"We are good but we miss you and your sister." I reply.

"I miss you both too, and Bane." I laugh.

"Are you getting your school work done?"

"Yes, but Grandpa says this new math is bullshit." She tells me.

"Dee, do not say that!" I hear my father-in-law call out in the background. "She's not wrong though!" I shake my head.

## PIECE BY PIECE

"Mom?" She whispers.

"Yeah, baby?" I say.

"Is the bad man going to hurt you?" She asks me, fear in her voice.

"No, Dee, he won't," I answer her confidently. I honestly do not know what he will do but I cannot let her know that.

"That is what Grandpa says. He says the bad man is a dumbass thinking that he can hurt you, especially with dad there."

"Dee! Do not say dumbass." I scold her. "Again, she is not wrong!" I hear my father-in-law through the phone. Lord, help, I pray to myself as I chuckle.

"I love you, Mom, and give Bane a hug for me!" I tell her I love her too.

My father-in-law then takes the phone, "Hey kid, how are things?" I tell him all that has happened since he picked up the girls. He is quiet for a bit, then says, "Cops cannot do anything yet, of course."

I respond, "No sir, they cannot." His voice turns grim, "Which means by the time they can, it will be too late."

"Pretty much," is all I can say.

"So this guy blames you for everything?" He asks.

"Seems that way."

"I have faith that you and my son will take care of it." He sounds so confident.

As if on cue, Rafe steps into our room with nothing but a towel around his waist. "We can." I reply to my father-in-law while drinking in the sight of my gorgeous husband. Fuck, he is so damn sexy, I think to myself.

"I will let you go, I think Jessie is holding Dee hostage, so I better go negotiate her terms."

I laugh and say, "Bye Dad," and we hang up.

"That was your dad, apparently our new tactical and gun safety experts." I tell Rafe, laughing. Rafe, still in nothing but his towel, leans against the door frame and gives a low chuckle. "That does not surprise me." All I can do is stare at him. How did

I get so lucky? I think to myself as I stare at him, remembering how we met.

When I met him at the age of twenty three, my life was nothing but trauma, anger, resentment, alcohol, and promiscuity. I never wanted to get married, let alone have kids. I could never trust a man enough to make that move with one. I wouldn't risk fucking a child's life up like mine was.

Then I met Rafe. I was at the bar with some friends, slamming shots of patron, then "Copper Head Road" came on and we all took off to go dance. When the song finished, I made my way back to our table where my friend Becky and her husband Steve were. Steve had brought a couple of his guy friends from work, one of them being Rafe.

My type was normally big, football player type looking men. Strong, tall, and tough men. Basically if I felt I could beat a guy's ass then he wasn't good enough for me. Blonde haired and blue eyes as well. So, when I met Rafe who was 5'11" and maybe 140 pounds, you and anyone who knew me would think I wouldn't even say hello to him. But there was something about Rafe. Something I could not explain drew me to him, pulled me to him. He was calm, quiet, and confident. His "I-don't-give-a-fuck" attitude was intriguing to me.

## PIECE BY PIECE

For his thin frame, he filled a pair of jeans very well. His shirt was tight enough to tell he was muscular, but not like gym-rat muscular. More like throwing hay bales all summer muscle, hard work muscle. His dark short hair was hidden under a baseball cap, but it was his eyes that did it. They were this blue-green color, like a tropical island ocean. I had never seen more beautiful eyes than his. I felt like he could see into my whole being and know everything there was to know, without me telling him a thing.

Steve introduced us as we all sat around the table, bullshitting. Rafe sipped some darker beer, while I kept up with my tequila. "I Cross My Heart" by George Strait came on. Steve grabbed Becky's hand dragging her to the dance floor. By that time, Steve's other two friends had headed home to their families. It was just Rafe and me at the table. Rafe stood up and comes around to my side, sticking out his sun tanned hand to me. "Dance with me," he said, looking at me with those eyes I could not look away from. It was a demand, not a question, and normally, that would set me off, but when he did it, I got nervous and giddy like a schoolgirl. "Are you asking me?" I say with sarcasm, half drunk. I couldn't just give in, even if he was gorgeous. I never take demands from men, I say to myself.

"No" was his only response, but his quiet smile gave him away. He knew I was stubborn and he would enjoy playing with me. Fucking Steve probably told him I was a uptight bitch. "Anna, dance with me," he said again, definitely not a question. I could tell by his face, he would not offer his hand again. I took his hand, saying nothing. What could I say? His hand was rough and warm, way bigger than mine. I imagined what they would feel like all over my body as we danced to the song, saying nothing to each other.

As we danced, it was not awkward or tense at all. One of my hands was on his shoulder; he took the other one and wrapped it around his neck. He placed both his hands around my waist, pulling me into him. *Damn it, he smells so good.* No cologne, just fresh shower scent and his natural smell. He felt even better than he smelled, we fit together so damn good.

The song ended, but he didn't let me go. "Shameless" by Garth Brooks came on next and we kept dancing. I stared at him, taking in and memorizing his features. Strong jaw, masculine, his skin showing he spent time outside a lot more than he did inside. His lips were full and look very inviting. He startled me back to the present, "What are you thinking?" He asked, looking into my eyes. *Why can't I stop looking at his mouth?*

"Nothing," I managed to reply. He snorted and gave me a beautiful grin.

"Liar."

I gave him a "fuck you" look. "Well, know it all, what do you think I'm thinking?" I snapped back at him. A full, arrogance-laced grin spread over his face.

"I think you're thinking that you want to kiss me."

I burst out laughing. "Oh I do, do I?"

"Yeah, you do." His grin got bigger. *Cocky bastard.* "You should," he said, looking me dead in the eyes. His eyes became an even darker shade of blue than they were originally.

I didn't know if I wanted to slap him or give him what he demanded. He didn't give me a choice. He framed my face with his hands and covered my mouth with his. That was no quick peck either. It was a deep, hot kiss; his tongue working its way slowly into my mouth to find mine. His lips were soft but firm.

"What are you thinking?" Rafe asks me, pulling me back from memory lane.

"Nothing," I reply.

"Liar," he shot back, grinning. I grinned back, biting my bottom lip.

"Know it all, what do you think I am thinking?"

He pushes himself off the door frame and slowly walks towards me, dropping the towel. "How about I show you what I think you're thinking?"

He falls asleep before me, exhausted from lovemaking, but I cannot sleep. I get up and walk to the kitchen to get some water. I stand at the sink, looking out the window. It is pitch black out. I close my eyes; bad things happen in the dark. I let out a breath and open the window, walking back to my bed, to my husband, to try and sleep.

## CHAPTER 15

*Then*

"Hey Anna!" I heard my name being called from across the gym. I smiled, "Hey Ben!" I jogged over to where Ben, Lisa, and a few others were. "Party at my house Saturday night, you in?" Ben asked me. I shrugged. "Should be alright, but more than likely I will have to bring dumbass Jack with me," I said, rolling my eyes. Ben and Lisa laughed. "Well, he is entertaining, I guess," Ben replied. I smacked him in the shoulder, "Glad you think so, asshole."

Saturday came, and as I predicted, I could only go if Jack took me. I needed a drink, badly. We pulled up and the party was already in full swing. I took off into the house, leaving Jack to fend for himself. I made it to the kitchen and Lisa squealed. "Yay! You're finally here!" She practically screamed as she hugged me.

# PIECE BY PIECE

"I need a drink," I told her, grabbing a red solo cup. I slammed its contents; Jack Daniels was becoming my favorite man. I grabbed another and slammed that one too. "Whoa, Anna, slow down," Lisa said, her voice full of concern. I just laughed it off. "I'll be fine, Lisa," I said casually as I took another shot.

We headed out to join the rest of the crowd. Taking a seat at the fire, Lisa and I quietly observed our fellow students and others we didn't know before she touched my arm. "Are you okay?" I took another swig. "Yeah, I'm golden, why?" I hiccupped. She continued, "Well, you normally don't drink at all, you know, because of your dad and all. Now you're knocking them back like they are water," she told me, her eyes full of worry and concern.

I studied her for a moment, debating whether I could tell her the truth. She had been my best friend, besides Alex, for five years by that point. She had been there for me when my dad bailed on me time and time again. She had seen Bud when he acted up, but never at his worst. That was a secret I could not risk getting out, not even with her.

I gave her a half grin. "I appreciate the concern, Lisa, really. Bud is up to the same shit, Jack is getting worse, and to top it off, I should be with my dad right now, but as you can see,

I'm not. So, right now, I want to forget everything for a bit." I hated seeing the pity in her eyes. She was an amazing friend, but her parents had always been together her whole life and they adored her. She did not fully understand at all what I was going through.

"Okay" was her only response. I finished my drink and felt it working its magic. "I'm going into the house for a bit, you coming?" She asked, standing up and taking a deep breath and letting it out. I shook my head, "Nah, I'll stay here a bit." We waved at each other and she headed inside the house.

All alone around the fire, I stared off into the flames. At fourteen years old, my life is already over, I think to myself. No one wanted me, like truly wanted me for me. I was willing to bet if I died, the only one who would care would be Josie. As I stared into the flames, I could hear her screams in my head. I could hear Bud's voice calling her names as he hit her repeatedly. I got instantly pissed just thinking about it, blood boiling. *No one will beat me or Josie again if I can help it.*

"Why are you here?" The question pulled me from my thoughts. I looked up and saw fucking Stacy. I gave her a shit-eating grin then turned back to the fire, ignoring her. "I said," she spoke again loudly, "Why the fuck are you here?" I let out a big

# PIECE BY PIECE

sigh and stood up to face her, people watching and whispering. I rolled my eyes. "Ben invited me, not that it's any of your fucking business." She scoffed, "Yeah, right! No one wants you here, no one fucking likes you!" She slurred and then hiccups.

"Whatever you say, Stacy," I rolled my eyes and turned to go back in the house to find Lisa when suddenly Stacy shoved me. "I heard you wanted to fight me, bitch!" Her words were slurred but laced with contempt. I waved my hand around. "In front of all these people?" I said sarcastically, signaling that there was no one around. "Fucking smartass!" She screamed as she shoved me again. This time, a crowd gathered around us. Stay calm, I think to myself. "I am not going to fight you, Stacy, you're drunk," I told her as I noticed Christian standing in the crowd. Then all the emotions hit me at once. "Fucking pussy! Fight me!" Stacy yelled as she shoved me a third time, and everything suddenly went black.

When I came to, Stacy was sitting on me, her hands pinning me down. "Anna! Stop! Are you done?" She cried, her hair hanging down, covering both our faces. It was so dark I couldn't see her face even though she was inches from me. "Yeah! Are you?" I screamed back at her. "Yeah, yeah, I'm done," she practically whispered. "Then get the fuck off me!" I practically spat at her. She let me go and I climbed to my feet.

# PIECE BY PIECE

The crowd was much bigger now, bigger than I remembered and everyone was quiet, just staring at me. I finally noticed the pain in my hands. I ran to the house, straight for the bathroom.

I felt physically sick when I looked at myself in the mirror. Blood covered my face, shirt, and my right hand. I quickly grabbed a washcloth and turned on the cold water. I began washing my face to see what the damage was. I had just gotten braces and Bud was going to beat me worse than Stacy did. I was shaking so badly I started crying.

Ben, and Stacy's brother, Max, came rushing into the bathroom. Ben spoke first, "Are you okay, Anna? That was the coolest thing I have ever seen!" As I looked at my face in the mirror, panic set in. "Ben? Is this not my blood?" I was bawling and shaking so badly that Ben grabbed me for a hug. "Its okay, its okay," he said, squeezing me tight. I looked him dead in the face. "Ben, where is she?" I pleaded with him. "She's upstairs, Mom is looking her over. You really did a number on her," he said calmly. Fuck. *How is that possible?* I had never been in a real fight before!

Max piped in. "You jacked her up real good, Anna. She didn't even get a hit in! What saved her was you slipping on the grass and falling. It was awesome! No one ever has stood up to her!" Panic was settling within me and I spoke in a rush. "Take me to her, please, Ben," He nodded and we headed upstairs.

We walked to the kitchen and Stacy was sitting at the kitchen table, a bag of ice to the right side of her face. Ben's mom was cleaning her up when they both looked at me. Ben stood between us as Stacy removed the ice from her face. *Oh my god, what have I done?*

Her right eye was already turning blue and purple, her lip swollen, a cut just under her right eye, and her nose still bleeding. I burst into tears. "Stacy, I am so sorry!" I sob, "I didn't mean it, I don't know what happened!" She cut me off. "I started it, Anna, this is on me," she said quietly. I stared at her, stunned. "I am sorry, Anna, for all of it," she said, getting up and sitting right back down with a wince. "Got my ankle rolled too," she said with an awkward laugh. I walked to where she was and we hugged immediately, apologizing again. *I need to get air.* Ben's mom gave me a reassuring smile, but it did not help my panic and fear of what I had done.

I found my way to Jack's car and sat in the passenger's seat, leaving the door open. My feet were still on the ground, my head in my hands. A few minutes later, three of Stacy's friends surrounded me. "What the hell, Anna! Why would you do that?"

The first girl yelled. "She was drunk! She didn't know what she was doing!" The second one yells next. I sprang to my feet, confident that these girls were going to jump me. "I fucking defended myself! I just talked with her! We are good!" I yelled back "You didn't have to go that far!" The third finally chimed in. I got pissed again. "If she had been the one to kick my ass, you all would be laughing about it right now! But because the tables have turned, I'm the fucking bad guy! So leave me the fuck alone before you three need ice packs to match hers!" They all gave me disdainful looks before turning around and walking away, whispering to each other rapidly. I let out a big sigh.

"When did you become such a badass?" I breathed in sharply. Christian. I was not in the right mindset to deal with him. "I'm not," I said, turning to face him. "I saw the whole thing, Anna. She didn't have a chance," he said, eyeing me suspiciously. I wanted so badly to run into his arms and disappear into the safety he gave me, the only safety I had known. I shrugged instead. "I don't remember any of it, I blacked out." He nodded, putting his hands in the pocket of his jacket. "Not going to lie, Anna, it was insane to watch. Seriously, where did you learn to fight like that?"

*How do I tell him I had no choice but to learn how to defend myself at a very young age?* I looked at the ground so he couldn't see my tears. "I didn't learn, I just reacted," I whispered. Before I could look up, he stood toe to toe with me, bringing my face up to look at him. *God, he feels so good.* Just that little touch broke my heart, knowing I couldn't have more. "Are you okay?" He asked me softly. I wanted to cry because of the tender look in his eyes. "I'm fine, I promise, Christian." He didn't let go, looking in my eyes the way he did, searching for any hints. I knew he could see right through me. "I'm here if you need me," he says, framing my face in both hands. I did need him. I needed him so bad that everyday without him was hell, but I couldn't tell him that. I nodded and he gave me a quick kiss before letting me go. I felt instantly cold, his warmth and safety gone. "Bye, Anna," he said, stepping back from me. I nodded, not being able to bring myself to speak.

## CHAPTER 16

*Now*

Todd sits in his chair, staring at me like I grew another head. I have just finished getting him caught up on everything that has been going on. "Anna, I cannot begin to imagine or understand what you and your family are feeling right now," he finally says. His voice has a tone of concern, not pity. I shrug and look at my hands, picking at my nails and the skin around them.

"I agree, the police can't do anything until you have solid proof that it is, in fact, him," he tells me as he shakes his head and leans forward on his desk, forearms resting on the top, fingers interlocked. "Have you brought it to the police's attention at least?" He asks. I take a deep breath and let it out before I answer. "Yeah, but they just told me what I already knew."

He nods. "So, what are you going to do?" I chuckle, shaking my head. "What can I do? Wait for him to fuck up, I guess, and he will." Todd looks me dead in the eyes. "And when he does?" I look back at him when I answer, not blinking. "When he does, I will handle it." Todd leans back in his chair, his hands now resting on the top of his head. "That is what worries me, Anna. I will be praying for you."

I leave Todd's office and head to my jeep, Bane at my side. I dig my keys out of my pocket and go to open the door when I see the glass everywhere, the windshield shattered. I walk around to the other side and find "I see you" scratched into the passenger door. Bane begins barking, his bark echoing through the parking garage. I grab the gun from its holster on my belt. I look around slowly, but nothing. I hush Bane and grab my cell phone next.

I call 911 to report the attack on my jeep and they are on their way. I move Bane away from the shattered glass and call Rafe. He beats me to it. "Anna?" I can't make out his voice; is he scared or mad or both? "We have a problem," he says calmly. *Fuck, now what?* "Your mom called, Anna, it's Josie," he says. Panic sets in immediately. "What happened?" I ask him, trying not to panic. "She's in the hospital, she tried to kill herself again," he tells me sympathetically. The shaking gets worse. *Damn it, Josie.*

Rafe continues. "Before you lose your shit, your mom says she is stable, she will need to go back to a rehab facility." I sigh. "Okay, I will call my mom. Rafe?" I say. "Yeah, baby?" He says. "We have more problems than that." I tell him as I hear the police sirens in the background. I stare at my jeep. "Well the jeep is damaged. The windshield is busted and "I see you" is scratched into the passenger door."

"That son of a bitch! I will kill him! Are you okay? Is Bane okay? Where are you?" He demands. "Calm down. I'm in Todd's parking garage. Bane and I are fine. Cops are already on their way." I tell him, my panic and anxiety calming down just by the sound of his voice. "Me too, baby." He tells me and hangs up.

Two hours later, we get home. The jeep is towed and the garage is cleaned up after informing Todd of what has happened. Of course, the security cameras show nothing but a hooded figure. We cannot make out who it is, even if I know who it is. Rafe grabs himself a beer and coffee for myself as I call my mom. "Oh, Anna! It is so much worse this time!" She answers the phone without even a hello. "Hello, Mom. Sorry, I would have called earlier but I had an issue with my jeep." I say, not acknowledging what she said. "I'm sorry, Anna, i'm freaking out, baby. What happened?" She says, calming down a little. I tell her what happened and how the cops are looking into it. "They have video from the cameras, but it doesn't really show anything at all," I tell her with a sigh.

"So, what is going on with Josie?" I ask her. She sniffles. "She took some pills, not sure what kind. They said a friend called in, but there is no evidence of who the friend is. The police found her in her apartment and there was a note, Anna." I close my eyes, trying to hold back my tears and anger. "What does it say, Mom?"

"Um, the police took it, they said when she is sent to the facility, someone would be reaching out to you since you are her primary," she says, her voice getting softer. "Okay, Mom, I'll take care of it." I tell her. "Anna, she is not your responsibility," my mom says, using the 'mom tone'.

A long time ago, my mom resented the fact that I was appointed primary, per Josie's choice. It ended in a big fight, but now she seems grateful that I can do what I do for Josie. "She is an adult now, Anna," she says, repeating herself for the thousandth time since Josie turned eighteen. "Just keep me updated and I will deal with the rest." I respond. We say our goodbyes and hang up.

"You want a drink?" I hear Rafe say from behind me. I shake my head. I don't really drink anymore. He comes up behind me, wrapping his arms around me. He's my safety. "Your mom is right, Anna. Josie is an adult now, you can not take care of her forever." He whispers as he rests his chin on my shoulder. I let out a deep breath. "I am all she has, Rafe, I am all she truly has." He squeezes me tighter, kissing my neck. "I know, baby. Have the facility email me the bill." *How did I get so lucky? I really do not deserve this man.*

I am awakened by my phone at 5:30 am. I check the caller ID and do not recognize the number, so I let it go to voicemail. The ding for my voicemail goes off and now I am up. Maybe it is Josie, or the hospital, or even the police with a new lead. I sit up in bed and hit play to listen to it. "Good morning, Anna. This is your father, you know, the one you do not claim anymore. I am aware you want nothing to do with me and I can say the same but we need to talk. Call me back. Please." The message cuts off. *What now?* I haven't spoken to this man in years, so what could possibly be so important he calls me at this time? I decide to wait to call him back. I have other things that need to be handled first, like a long, hot shower followed by some strong ass coffee.

# CHAPTER 17

*Then*

Sophomore year was a blur. Mostly because I spent the whole time pretty much drunk off my ass. My grades started slipping, Bud got worse, and Jack followed suit. By the end of that year, I was already labeled a "whore" even though I had never had sex. Sure, I flirted a lot, but could not bring myself to go any further than the occasional make-out session.

I also became well-known for being mouthy and rebellious. I did not care; no one knew me, the real me. No one knew about what I was going through with Bud and Jack. So, my philosophy was "fuck it." People could think what they want and you could not change their mind. Not that I wanted to. People left me alone for the most part because of how I portrayed myself and kept them at arm's length. It also made it easier to hide just how bad it had become at the house. When people saw bruises, they assumed I had been in another fight at some party. Who was I to tell them differently? No one would have believed me anyway. They never did.

The summer between my sophomore and junior years was rough, probably the worst one from my childhood. I was at a party with some "friends" at a house I had never been to before. All I knew was that the guy who lived there was just a few years older than me and lived with his mom and brother. He didn't go to our school; he had been kicked out of every school he went to. At least that was what I was told. Halfway through the night, my so-called friend supposedly got a call and had to leave, promising to be back soon. I sat on the couch, looking at the people partying at a distance. "It's just you and me, baby," the guy whose house it was sat down next to me. "I'm *not* your baby, and I need to go home. Now," I said, trying to hide the fear in my voice. I was only fifteen years old and had never been in such a situation with someone I did not know.

"Oh, come on, hang with me just a little longer!" He purred at me as he put his arm around me. He made me feel so uncomfortable but was easily twice my size, at least as tall as Christian, but not as strong-looking as him. "I want to show you something," he persisted. "Come with me." He grabbed my hand, pulling me into the hall from the couch in the living room. Panic set in. *What do I do? Do I fight him and try to run? Do I go along with him in hopes he will just let me go?* I realized I couldn't fight him; there was no way I could have won.

"Can I use your phone? I need to call my mom," I asked him as we stopped in front of a door. "Come here," he demanded, ignoring my request to call my mom. "Why?" I said, trying to pull free from him. His grip got tighter and he pulled me into a bedroom. I started getting really scared, hoping my friend would come back any minute. He pointed to the bed and said, "I hear you're a rebel, is that true? On one of these, at least?" I shook my head. He laughed, "Yeah, you are. Let's see how rebellious you really are."

He grabbed me and began to try and kiss me, basically shoving his tongue down my throat. I wanted to puke. He pushed me onto the bed and began pulling my shirt up. His weight pinned me to the bed and I couldn't move. "What the fuck are you doing! Get off me!" I yelled, hitting him with all my strength. He let out an ugly laugh. "What do you think? We are going to have a little fun." I practically growled at him, "No! I don't want to, let me go! Get off of me!" I pushed him and kicked my legs.

"You're a tease, you know that?" He joked, pinning my arms down with his hands. He started grinding his hips into mine and I could feel him against me. Then, it fully registered what he planned to do. "Seriously, let me go! Please!" I cried, the tears starting to fall. He sighed, "I wanted to show you something cool, remember?" He said, still not moving off of me. I stared at him like he had lost his damn mind. He reached into the bedside table, still not moving off me or giving me a chance to move.

He pulled out a condom and my eyes went wide. "I said no!" I screamed but he laughed, his voice creeping me out. "Not that, well not *just* that." He reached further into the drawer and pulled out a pistol. *Fuck!* I went completely still. "Cool, isn't it?" He said mockingly. "Um, yeah," I stammered in fear. He held it in front of my face, twirling it around for me to see all of it. "A lot of girls think it's hot, don't you?" He said as he set it on the nightstand. "Not really," I answered honestly, still scared, "I was leaving." He ignored me and started unbuttoning my jeans, grinning at me. "Not yet, we haven't had fun yet. You will do what I want, only *then* you go."

"I said *no*!" I screamed and he covered my mouth. "Let's not make this *not fun*!" He whispered, grabbing the gun. "This means yes, right? I mean, no one has ever said no to me when I have this."

He set the gun back down and grabbed the condom. "Better safe than sorry," he said with a disgusting smirk. I was in full-blown panic mode by that point. I had never had sex in my life. I was terrified. I had plans to wait and had dreams to wait for the person I wanted to give myself to. He didn't hesitate and thrust hard into me. I screamed as he covered my mouth again. It hurt so bad. "Shhh. Good girl. You love it, don't you? Fuck, you're tight, especially for a slut!" He groaned. His breath was disgusting. "Stop, please!" I begged. "Shhh, just enjoy it," he cooed as he covered my mouth with his.

His pace got quicker, making the pain worse. I closed my eyes tight. Think of something good, I thought to myself. An image of Christian appeared in my mind. My tears fell harder. I am so sorry, Christian, I thought to myself. I felt his body start to stiffen. "Fuck, yes, here I come, baby!" He said as he moaned, his sweat covering me. Don't puke, I told myself. He pulled out as fast as he shoved in. Getting dressed, he looked at me and grinned. "I am starving. Get yourself together before someone comes back," he snickered and left the room, humming to himself.

## PIECE BY PIECE

    I just laid there for a minute. I turned my head to the side and saw it. The gun. He left it out. I got up and got myself together when I noticed blood on the sheet. It still hurt like hell and the tears were still falling. I started getting angrier as I came to terms with what had just happened. I grabbed the gun, feeling its weight in my hand. *The one innocent thing I had left, he stole it!* I left the room, following the noise of the TV, the gun behind me in my right hand. He was sitting on the couch, eating a sandwich like nothing happened. I pointed the gun at him when he looked up. "You're going to shoot me?" He asked mockingly, not even flinching. I was shaking with anger. "I told you no!" I growled through clenched teeth. He sighed and rolled his eyes. "You wanted it, you liked it, just like every other slut. Do not pretend you didn't enjoy it. *I* did." I put both hands on the gun, and without thinking for a second longer, squeezed the trigger but all I heard was a click. I did it again, with the same outcome. He burst out laughing and said, "It's not loaded, you dumbass. You really think I would leave a loaded gun out?" He laughed again. Not knowing how to react, I dropped the gun to the floor and took off, out of the apartment and into the street. His laughter was echoing in my head. I kept running till I couldn't run anymore. I veered off the road behind a tree and puked.

## PIECE BY PIECE

My mom thought I was staying the night at a friend's house. She had no clue where I was. I walked to the gas station a few miles away to borrow their phone. I didn't even know who to call. *Alex! I can call her.* In twenty minutes, she reached there and we headed to her house. I just wanted a shower and to sleep.

"Feel like going to a party?" She asked me in a bored tone. "Is there going to be alcohol?" I asked numbly. She laughed and said, "Duh, dude." She had no clue as to what had happened to me and I never let anything on. "Sure, let's go, I want to get fucked up," I told her. So, we headed to another party and I got fucked up.

A week after that horrible night, Alex and I were driving around once again, just listening to music. We saw a group of cars we recognized as belonging to our friends lined up in the mall parking lot. We pulled in to visit them. A good friend of mine, Steve, was there. I had been friends with him for seven years by then and I hadn't seen him all summer.

"Hey, Anna!" Steve yelled, giving me a hug, "How have you been?" He asked, pulling back from our hug. "Not too bad, how are you?" I lied through my teeth. He shrugged and grinned. "Not bad, not bad at all. What are you two troublemakers up to?" He joked, giving me a gentle shove. Alex piped in, "I got to go meet up with Kyle and I was going to take Anna home first, then we saw you guys." Kyle was her new boyfriend.

Steve looked at me. "Do you want to go home, Anna?" He asked me. He knew I didn't and also knew why. "Not really, but she is my ride," I answered his question. "You can hang out with me for a bit then. We can catch up; I miss hanging out with you!" He offered. At first, I got scared at the thought of being alone again with a guy. *What if?* I mentally slapped myself. *This is Steve, I have been alone with him a million times and he has always been amazing.* "That sounds better than going to the house," I said.

Acknowledging the agreement, Alex took off to meet Kyle. Steve looked at me. "Feel like driving around?" I nodded and we climbed into his car. We drove around, catching up on each others' lives. "So, what exactly is going on with you, Anna? And don't say 'nothing'. I have known you for years and I know that is bullshit." He looked at me out of the corner of his eye while he drove down a side road. If there was anyone I could confide in, it was Steve. Even more than Alex and Lisa. He was my first kiss and the first guy to look at me as more than just one of the guys before I met Christian. We decided a long time ago we were better off as friends though, and neither of us wanted to risk our friendship.

# PIECE BY PIECE

I looked out the window. "Tell me, Anna," he urged softly. I sighed, wringing my hands in my lap. "I'm sure you have heard all about my new reputation in this piece of shit town." He nodded slowly. "Yeah, I have heard. It's bullshit, of course, because I know you." I sat quietly, not knowing what to say next, or at least, how to say it. "That's not all, is it, Anna? Is it Bud? Jack?" He asked, concern filling his voice. I chuckled humorlessly and said, "They are *always* bothering me, Steve. That's nothing new."

He pursed his lips, nodding. "That's true. Then what is it? The lies about you?" I shrugged, "I can handle that too."

"But you are still a virgin, they don't know that about you..." I burst into tears before he could finish. He pulled the car over, turning me towards him, grasping my shoulders. "Anna? Are you not a virgin anymore? It's okay, you can tell me, you know that." I looked around and noticed that we were on a dirt road out by the river that ran through town. It was my favorite place.

He turned my head back to him gently with his hand. "Who was it, Anna? You wanted to wait till you got married. Was it Christian? I will kill him!" He exclaimed, anger clear in his tone. I shook my head. "No, Steve, it was not Christian. I wish it was, though. I wish it was Christian so much it hurts." Steve stared at me for what seemed like forever, processing what I was telling him. "Who then, Anna?" He asked again gently. I mumbled through the tears. "You wouldn't know him. Hell, even I don't know him," I confessed before I realized I had said too much.

"What in the fuck does that mean, Anna?" He pressed. I turned back to the window. *How can it be so gorgeous out there when I feel so hideous?* Steve broke my thoughts by asking me quietly, "Did you want to, Anna?" I lowered my head, shaking it. "Fuck!" He yelled. "I will fucking kill that son of a bitch! Who is he? Tell me, Anna!" He demanded. I winced at his outburst; I had never seen Steve so mad before. He realized how his outburst affected me and immediately reeled back. "I am sorry, Anna," he said softly, resting a hand on my shoulder. "I didn't mean to get mad at you at all." I nodded in understanding, wiping the tears away. "Tell me what happened, Anna. Please." I took a deep, shaky breath and proceeded to tell him everything, not leaving anything out. When I finished, panic set in immediately. "You cannot tell anyone, Steve! Please! No one would believe it anyway with my reputation!" He scoffed but I knew it wasn't directed at me. I continued to plead anyway. "I'm serious, Steve, please! I will be fine," I said, trying to convince the both of us.

"Anna, your father is a piece of shit. Bud and Jack abuse you relentlessly. Now you have to deal with this? Fuck, your view of men must be really fucked up," he said angrily, but the look in his eyes held a different emotion. I nodded. "But I know you're not like that, Steve, I'm not that disillusioned and blind. You're a good guy. You're my friend and the only guy I have ever fully trusted, always." His sad smile touched my heart. He then cleared his throat and said, "I hate that your first experience happened like that, Anna. You should have had a choice, with someone you loved and trusted, but it was robbed from you." I started crying again, the tears falling but no noise coming out. "I am terrified of anyone touching me, Steve," I said, horror taking over my skin.

Steve took my hand, leaning towards me just a little bit. "I wish you loved me, Anna, so I can show you how it is supposed to be," he said, looking deep into my eyes. "How is it supposed to be?" I asked, confused. He gave me a sad smile. "Sex is supposed to feel good, Anna," he said as I scoffed. "Seriously, it is, and it does," he persisted. "Have you been with anyone at all who made you feel good when they touched you? Feel special? To the point that you could physically feel it in your body?"

I must have been looking really confused, because he elaborated. "Butterflies in your stomach? An overwhelming sense of happiness when you are with them or when you even think about them? Tingling in certain parts of your body? Heartbeat skips and speeds up?" I nodded. Christian was all I could think about. "Okay, now add sex, and it is ten times better," he told me, squeezing my hands. He continued. "That is how you should feel when you decide it is time."

I took a minute to process what he told me. "I will never feel that again, Steve. I can't," I said so quietly I doubted if he even heard me. "Christian? It is him, isn't it, who makes you feel that way?" Steve said. He knew me so damn well. "Is it that obvious?" I asked him. He laughed, sitting back in his seat, "Yeah, it is. Why can you never feel that way again? Because of what that motherfucker did to you? Or whatever Christian did?" I shook my head. "Christian did nothing wrong, it was all my fault." He raised his eyebrows and said, "I doubt that. He is not so innocent." I looked straight at him. "In this case, he was."

"So why did you break up with him if he did nothing wrong?" He asked me. "I didn't have a choice, and I don't want to talk about it, I have talked enough anyway." He looked at me for a moment longer before he nodded and started driving again.

# PIECE BY PIECE

We drove around town some more and the sun began to set. We rode in silence for a long time and I used that time to think about what Steve said to me. "You hungry?" He asked, breaking my train of thought. "Not really, but I should probably eat something, I guess," I answered him. Between what had happened in the last few weeks and the amount of alcohol I had been consuming, I hadn't eaten much. Steve looked at me and nodded. "Yeah, you should. Want to go see what my mom is cooking?" He suggested and my spirit lifted a little. "Yeah! She's an amazing cook! I haven't seen her in a while either."

"Okay then, let's go," he said and headed to his house. A wave of excitement ran through me; his mom was an awesome woman. She was so bubbly and welcoming.

We got to his house and walked right to the kitchen. His mom gasped in surprise when she saw me. "Oh, Anna! It has been so long!" She cried while giving me a hug. She held me at arm's length and scanned me thoroughly. "Girlie, you need some meat on your bones!" I laughed. "Yes ma'am."

"Well, good thing I have food in the fridge. Just heat it up, you two. I have to go. I'm meeting Steve's dad for our date!" She said excitedly, giving us each a hug goodbye and then left.

# PIECE BY PIECE

We heated up the homemade lasagna and sat down on the couch. "You still like horror movies?" Steve asked me while taking a big bite of food. "Of course!" I answered in between my bites of food. We picked "The Ring" and started the movie. I did like horror movies, though I kept my eyes closed or covered through most of them. When it ended, Steve laughed at me and asked, "How can you love horror movies and then keep your eyes closed the whole time?" I shrugged. "No clue," I said, laughing awkwardly, "but I do love them!"

Chuckling, Steve checked his watch. "Do I need to get you home?" I checked mine; it was 7:30 p.m., so I shook my head. "My mom thinks I'm staying at Alex's tonight, after the party we were supposed to go to."

"So, I'm taking you to a party, huh?" He asked but I shook my head again. "We just told our parents that so we could do whatever we wanted without them up our asses." He shoved me playfully. "You little rebel!" I laughed. "You can just drop me off in town if you have other plans," I suggested, not looking at him.

"No plans. We can watch another movie. I can make some popcorn," he said, grabbing the remote. I sat up on the couch, leaning my forearms on my knees. "Actually, Steve, I was wondering…" I said shyly, not knowing if what I was about to ask him would freak him out. "Yeah?" He answered, still browsing through the movie list. *Fuck. How do I ask him? Do I even really want to?*

"Um, remember our conversation today, about sex?" I couldn't even look at him when I asked him that. He turned to me with a confused look. "Yeah. Do you have more questions? You don't need to be scared or shy about this, Anna." He said in a reassuring tone. I knew I could trust him; I could feel it. "What do you want to know?" He pressed gently. I took a deep breath. *Here it goes.*

"Would you, um, maybe, want to show me?" I almost whispered, licking my lips because I was so nervous. It took him a minute to process what I was asking him. His eyes went wide as he fully understood what I was saying. "You want me to show you what sex is supposed to be like?" His tone gave nothing away, making it impossible to detect what he was thinking or feeling. *Fuck, can I find a hole to crawl into now?* I just nodded. He let out a breath and said, "Anna, you should-"

"Choose someone I care about and trust?" I cut him off. He nodded slowly "My choice, right?" I said and he nodded again. I couldn't back out and I didn't want to. "I choose you, Steve. Show me. I do care about you, and I do love you, just not in the way you think," I rambled. "I understand if you don't want to, but all I can think about and feel is that guy's sickening body, his smell, the pain, and I want it to stop. I want to know the good feelings, Steve, to know sex as a good thing." I let out a breath as I finished, letting him have all the time he needed to process the bombshell I had dropped on him.

He finally spoke. "Do you want a relationship out of this or what?" I thought about it and then said, "Honestly, no. I just want to know that when I was given the choice, it was with someone I will never regret choosing, someone who would never hurt me or spread rumors about me. That is you, Steve. But as I said, if you don't want-" He cut me off, "I want to." My stomach flipped. "You do?" His hand framed my face again, "Yes. The fact that you trust me to do this means a lot to me, Anna. I just want you to be sure." I covered his hands with mine. "I *am* sure. Please. Make me forget."

# CHAPTER 18

*Now*

On the third ring, my sperm donor answers. "This is Sean." *What do I call him?* "Uh, hey Sean, this is Anna. You called?" Silence. "Sean?" I ask, thinking he hung up. "Yeah, hey. So, um, we need to talk, kid." He finally says. I hate when he calls me 'kid'. I roll my eyes. "Okay Sean, what about?" I can feel the irritation setting in. "Can we talk in person?" He asks. I close my eyes, feeling a migraine starting. I let out a breath and say, "I would rather not, Sean." He never wanted to see me as a kid, so why see him as an adult?

"Yeah, okay, fine." He says with an attitude in his tone, showing that he is not pleased. *That makes the two of us, old man.* "What is so important, Sean?" I ask, cutting right to the reason for this bullshit call. "Apparently, Jack has been here." He answers. *Fucking hell.* He continues. "I am guessing he doesn't know we are not on speaking terms. He talked to Shelly."

Shelly is Sean's newest wife. She also is the reason Sean and I don't talk anymore. "Did she tell him where to find me?" I am about to lose my shit. I can practically see her telling him everything just to spite me. "God, Anna! No! Despite what you may think, she is not that cruel." His irritation resounds in his tone. I roll my eyes  Yeah, she is, I think to myself. "Well, did she tell him we haven't spoken, let alone seen each other in years?" I ask him. "Basically, yeah, in a nutshell." He answers.

"What is that supposed to mean, Sean? What did she say exactly? Not basically?" I snap. "Look, I called because I thought you should know, that's all, not to get bitched at." He snaps back. I take a deep breath and try to control myself. "Sean, he has been stalking me and has vandalized my jeep. I need to know what was said. Please." Silence. After a few seconds that seem like many minutes, Sean responds. "Fuck, Anna, I had no idea." *No shit, Sherlock, because you bailed on me again.*

"Are you okay? Are the girls okay?" He asks. "What was said to Jack, Sean?" I demand. He sighs. "You won't even tell me how my grandchildren are?"

"No, you told me to fuck off, Sean. You said I was a hateful and ungrateful bitch, remember that? You have been in and out my entire life. More out than in. My girls will never know that hurt, therefore, they will not know you. So, either tell me what was said or hang up and never call me again." By the time I finish chewing out his ass, I am shaking. The line goes dead. *Figures.*

"Let me guess, he hung up," I spin around to see Rafe standing behind me. "Yeah." I say as I let out my breath. *Why do I let him get to me? I am used to this with him. This is nothing new.* I used to envy the girls who had daddies who cherished them. Now, I have Derek; he is my dad. He will never leave me or do what Sean has done to me my entire life. What I said to Sean was true. My girls will never wonder why grandpa left again and again. They will never know how it feels to have him make promises he will not keep or pawn their things for money. My girls will especially never know what it is like to go to him for help or safety just to be called a liar or let one of his many women be verbally and mentally abusive.

"Why are you crying, Anna?" Rafe says softly. "He isn't worth your tears."

"For so long, Rafe, I wanted to be a daddy's girl, to come first, no matter what. To have him at my games, take pictures with me at prom. Go to the father-daughter dances," I let out a hollow laugh and continue. "To threaten to kill any guy who hurts me. I will never know what that is like. To depend on my dad, for anything." Rafe hugs me. "You have that now, with Derek, don't you? He may not have been there when you needed it most, but he is here now, trust me on that." He grinned, squatting down in front of me. I laugh again, wiping my tears. Rafe is right, as always. It took a few years or more for Derek to trust Rafe. When Dee was born, Derek was there and told Rafe that if he was anything like Sean, then even God himself wouldn't even be able to find his body. He meant it too. Piece by piece, I think to myself and smile.

After reassuring me, Rafe heads to work and I walk out to our deck with a blanket and a cup of coffee, Bane settling down at my feet as I sit. *Fucking nightmares.* This time, I was in our bed and something or someone pulled me from my bed to the floor. I couldn't see anything but I could feel the hands and the pressure as I slammed into the baseboards. I couldn't move; something was holding me in place. Under my bed, I saw it. A solid black figure crouched down like a panther ready to pounce, but the body was human-like, contorted to look like a scared cat. With red glowing eyes and a nasty smile that showed sharp fangs, its movements were slow, creepy, and stalker-like. It was laughing at me. I tried to lunge at it, but I was pinned against the baseboards. Its laughing turned to a cackle and got louder, deafening. Rafe was still asleep on the bed above it. "Fucking pussy!" I yelled at it. "You have to keep me pinned against this wall because you know if you let me go, I will fuck you up and that scares you!" It growled. I lunged again and it let me go. I rushed under the bed, almost like I was thrown at it. Everything went black and then I woke up. Rafe was still sleeping as I tried to catch my breath.

I finish my coffee and bow my head. "God, I do not know your plan and I am feeling lost. What should I do? If I do what I feel is right, then I will fail you. If I do nothing, I might die, or worse, something could happen to Rafe or my girls." I am sobbing now. "Guide me to do what needs to be done, what your will is. Most of all, Lord, keep my Jojo safe. Especially from herself." I wipe my tears and get up. I need a run.

I put my running shoes on. Bane, knowing what's going on, starts bouncing and barking. "Yes, you are going too, my sweet boy. I cannot go without you," I say to him as I smile and rub his head. I always joke to Rafe that if Bane was a man, Rafe wouldn't have a chance in hell with me. Rafe rolls his eyes every time. "Worst gift I ever got you," Rafe would say. I grin to myself, thinking about how much I love that man.

## PIECE BY PIECE

We head to our regular running trail and I can't stop the memories that overcome me. I had an image of me at five years old, with my basketball team at our first game. Sean was there, screaming, "That's my girl! Hustle!" I wanted to make him proud of me so much. Then, my mind replayed a memory of Mom and Sean fighting because we were moving after her marriage to Bud. "You can't take her! She needs her dad!" Sean yelled. "She needs a dad who isn't a drunkard with more women than money!" I cried; I didn't want to leave my daddy. I was his little slugger. Bud picked me up and carried me out of Sean's apartment. "Come on, kid, you do not need to hear this."

I set my pace on the trail, no one on it but me and Bane. The memories keep coming. I was on my first flight to see my dad after the move. "Be brave, my girl, okay?" My mom said, "The nice staff will take care of you and make sure you get to your dad."

"Okay, mommy!" I was so excited to see Sean. I got on the plane and a few hours later, we touched down. I was so excited I could not sit still. I was the last one off and I was practically jumping up and down. I saw Sean and took off at full speed. "Daddy!" He picked me up. "Hey, slugger!"

"Are we going on vacation?" My little self asked him. "Uh, no, I got to work, slugger, so you get to spend that time with grandma and grandpa at the farm!" He told me, carrying me through the airport. I liked that idea. They spoiled me, especially Grandpa! "Um, Anna, baby," Sean said to me as he set me down, "I want you to meet someone." He pointed to a woman standing at the luggage claim. "This is Karen, we are going to get married." He smiled at me. She bent down to my height and said, "Hi, slugger!"

"Only Daddy calls me that." I snapped at her. "Anna! Be nice." Sean chided me. Karen stood up and took Sean's hand. I did not like her, even at my young age.

Bits and pieces come back to me as I try to keep up with the pace. Sean married Karen. Karen got knocked up. A boy, Grayson. My half-brother, they told me. Now Sean had his son. Karen became a hateful bitch to me. She got knocked up again, a few years later. Another boy, Kris. Me telling Sean that Bud beat me. Karen called me a liar and that I wanted Sean to myself so I made up lies to get him to take me from my mom. She didn't want me. Sean stopped paying child support and Bud used that as ammo to tell me that my own father did not care about me, that no one did and ever will.

## PIECE BY PIECE

I get to the top of the trail on the cliff and scream. I then take a look at the gorgeous scenery. God is a serious artist. Bane sits at my side, panting. My thoughts still come in waves. Sean leaves Karen. She got caught cheating, and then he did. Within less than a year, both got remarried. Shelly and her three girls joined in. Jennifer, Jaylynn, and Justine all live with him.

My cell phone goes off, pulling me from the painful memory lane, back to reality. Rafe. That is weird, he has only been gone an hour or so. "Hey babe, what's up?" I ask him. "Where are you?" He asks, his voice angry and cold. "Running, why? What's wrong?" I ask. What did I do? Why is he mad at me? I try to think of anything I may have done to set him off but quickly realize that's my insecurities and trauma speaking. "That motherfucker was at Dee's school, Anna." *Oh god, no.* "What? When?" I stammer. "Get home now!" He demands. "Rafe! Is she okay?" I scream at him. Bane whimpered. "She's fine, but we got to go to the school," he says, his tone clipped. "I'll be there in less than twenty minutes, I'm on top of the cliff," I tell him. "I will have the truck ready," with that, he hangs up. I reach for my gun; it is there, in its holster. I know it is but feeling it makes me feel better. I take off for home. I bet I will beat my record by a long shot.

Sure enough, I do. Less than twenty minutes later, I am at the house. Rafe is in the truck with it running. I open the back passenger door. "Load up, Bane," I command him. Bane jumps in, excited to be going for a truck ride. I climb in front with Rafe. He hands me my cigarettes. "Thanks," I say as I light one. "Figured you would need it," he says, looking at the windshield. We haul ass to the school.

Before Rafe can even get the truck in park, I am out and running towards the school. I run past the cop car and my father-in-law's truck. One of the teachers meets me at the door. "Come in, Mrs. Garrison, everyone is in my classroom." She tells me, leading me down the hall. I walk into the room and see my girls playing on the reading rug by the projector. The principal is sitting at the teacher's desk, facing my in-laws who are sitting at the little kids' table. A police officer is standing at the corner of the room, arms crossed over his chest so he can see the entire room and everyone in it.

Rafe catches up to me and our girls jump up screaming, "Mommy! Daddy!" I am on my knees, holding both my babies. I silently thank God for watching over them and keeping them safe. All the adults stand to face us. "Mr. and Mrs. Garrison, please have a seat and we can discuss this," the principal tells us, gesturing towards the table Rafe's parents were sitting at.

"Mom, can you take Jessie for a walk around the school?" Rafe asks his mom. "Of course. Jessie! Come with Mimi so Dee can talk with mommy and daddy." Jessie takes her hand, they leave the room, and the teacher shuts the door.

The principal starts talking but I put my hand up to stop him. "Dee, baby, tell me what happened." I ask her. "Mrs. Garrison, I can–" the principal cuts in. "My wife asked my daughter a question, you can wait till she asks you one." Rafe snaps in a tone that even has his father taken aback. The cop adjusts himself, to let it be known he was still there. Rafe looks at Dee. "Go on, baby girl, it's okay, you're not in any trouble at all," he tells her in a much softer tone.

Dee looks at every adult in the room before she focuses back on me and her dad. "Well, it happened at recess. Hannah and I were playing by the fence and this man came up and called my name." Fuck, he knows everything, I think to myself. "I have never seen him before. He said he was mom's brother and that he was here to pick me up so we could go see you." As I'm listening to her, I realize that I am shaking. *I am going to fucking kill him and ask forgiveness after.* Dee keeps going. "I told him he was a liar, Mom. He laughed at me. He had a weird laugh too. Then he told me that you probably told me to tell him that. He said he had to get me first, then my sister." Rafe cusses, running his hands down his face. "What?" I ask her, visibly shaking now. "Hannah grabbed my arm and started to pull me away. She told him he was a creepy pervert, whatever that means. He got mad and demanded I go with him right away. Hannah and I ran to get Miss Anderson. When I looked back, he just smiled and waved at me. It was creepy." I hug her immediately. "Oh, Dee, you did the right thing! You and Hannah are so smart!" Rafe turns to the police officer. "So, what can you do now?" The officer replied, "I already got her statement on recording. I spoke with Miss Anderson and got her statement as well. She said the man had on a black hoodie and from where she was, she could not make out any features. The girls could not really describe him either."

"So, what can you do then?" I ask him sternly. "We have guys out right now looking around, but the description is not much to go off of. I need to know why this guy is targeting you, Mrs. Garrison." I let out a deep breath. "Well, officer, how much time have you got? Because this will take some time," I tell him.

The teacher, principal, Rafe's dad, and Dee leave the room so I can get the officer caught up on Jack. Two hours later, the officer looks like he has a migraine. He lets out a deep sigh. "This goes way above my pay grade and rank, Mrs. Garrison. The problem we face now is that there is no solid proof that the stalker is, in fact, Jack." Rafe swears and starts pacing the room.

The officer looks at both of us, "Look, Mr. and Mrs. Garrison, I am not happy about this either. I have a wife and young kids myself. I would want his head on a silver platter if this was happening to my family."

"I don't need the platter, just his head," Rafe says. The officer holds both hands up to get Rafe to settle down. "I understand, but the law is the law. I am going to take this to my captain right away, let's see what he says. In the meantime, keep the girls in their routine, let him think you do not care, or even acknowledge he did anything. If he is who you say he is, he will mess up and we will get to him."

"Or I will," I tell him. "I'm going to pretend that I did not hear that, ma'am," the officer says with a smile.

We head out to meet with Rafe's parents and the girls. The officer talks to the principal a bit more, but I drown out whatever they are saying. I am so pissed that I can't hear, think, or feel anything but the darkness creeping up on me. I silently pray, "God, help me please."

# CHAPTER 19

*Then*

Junior year was rough for me. My drinking became almost constant. I learned that a Gatorade bottle half full of actual Gatorade and half vodka was unnoticeable to the teachers. I did everything I could to be near Christian. I often flirted in front of him with other guys to get his attention, but really to keep him thinking I did not want him. He could never know he still owned my heart. It was better that way. Just about every guy I was accused of sleeping with was a lie, but trying to tell the truth never got me anywhere but beaten and alone. Every day, I would find a way to see Christian. The pain I felt every day was slowly killing me. I would dream day and night of telling him the truth and how I wished it would turn out.

## PIECE BY PIECE

My fantasies were expansive. In a particular fantasy, Christian and I were at his house, the snow coming down like heavy rain. "I don't want to take you home, Anna," he whispered to me as we snuggled in his bed. "I don't want you to, either," I said as the tears fell. He sat up, looking down at me. "Woah, baby, what's wrong?" He asked me as he pulled me closer. He was so damn strong, stronger than anyone I knew. He was my safety blanket.

There was a knock on the door. I hated it. "Hey, Anna, your mom is on the phone," I heard Mrs. O'rion say. We got up and headed to the living room, holding Christian's hand and walking just behind him. I saw his mom on the phone and she looked upset. "Oh, of course, I understand. Yes, I agree," she said, looking at me. "Okay, here she is." She handed me the phone.

"Hey, Mom," I said to her. "If I find out she was sleeping in his room, I swear to god..." I heard Bud yelling in the background. "Mom?" I asked. "Shut up, Bud. Hey, honey. Mrs. O'rion and I both agree that no one should be driving in this weather, it's just too dangerous," my heart did a flip, "so you are just going to stay the night there." My face lit up. Christian's mom had already told him because he was grinning wide. "But..." My mom cut me off and continued. "You will be sleeping in his sister's room, you understand me?"

"Give me the fucking phone!" Bud snapped, taking the phone from my mom. "You fucking listen to me and listen good. You will do as I say or else..." My face fell, I wanted to cry. Christian looked at me, trying to figure out what was wrong. "Do you hear me? I will follow through with my promise!" I looked at Christian. I had had enough of this. My whole world was standing right in front of me and I would not let Bud take him from me. "Shut the fuck up, Bud!" I screamed into the phone. Christian and his mom stared at me; his dad got out of his chair to stand by me.

Bud growled into the phone. "What did you just say to me, girl?" I put him on speakerphone so they could all hear him. "I didn't stutter, Bud, you heard me! You can make your threats, you can even beat me some more," I yelled, my tears falling. Christian and his dad looked pissed. *Shit, here we go.* "But you will not tell me who I can or can't love. Try and follow through on your threats and see what happens!" I could hear his blood boiling over the phone. "I am going to fucking –" I interrupted. "What? Huh, Bud? You're going to come over here in this snowstorm and beat me again? Is it going to be open-handed or a closed fist this time? Since I know how both feel, can I choose?" His booming voice was loud enough for all to hear. "You little bitch! You think all those bruises and fat lips were bad? Wait till I get a hold of you!"

"By the time you get your stupid ass over here, Christian's family will know the entire story and so will the police. They're not fans of yours, by the way." With that, I hung up on him, angrily.

I looked at all three people who were staring at me. Through the tears, I said, "You may want to sit down for this." By the time I finished, Christian's mom was crying and his dad was pacing. Christian was looking out the living room window. "I am so sorry," I said, sobbing as well. Mr. O'rion was across the room but made it to me in probably two steps. I flinched; I couldn't help it. His face softened as he said, "Anna, I didn't mean to scare you, please. You need to know that you did nothing wrong, this is that piece of shit's fault." He pulled me into him for a hug and squeezed me tight. He never really talked to me a lot before, so I was in shock at his reaction. "He will never hurt you again," he said firmly as he let me go.

"I am going to kill him," Christian finally spoke. His dad turned to him. "Son, do you love her? Like really love her?" I couldn't look at Christian. I felt the rejection coming "More than my own life, Dad. She is my life." I looked at him in shock, hope filling every part of me. Christian turned to me. "Anna, you are my life. I love you so much." I run across the room toward him and launch myself into his arms, hanging on for dear life. "I love you too, Christian!" I started bawling. I buried my face in his neck. He smelled and felt so perfect. Mr. O'rion looked at Christian. "Then your job, son, is to protect her and you can't do that in prison."

The phone rang again. "I will be answering this," Mr. O'rion said, grabbing the phone. "Hello?" He said, looking at me. "Bud, I think you and I are going to need to chat, face-to-face." He looked mad and raised his voice. "No! You will listen to me! We all heard you earlier talking to her! So, you can say she is lying till you are blue in the face but she is safe here. Apparently, more than she is at your house. We will talk when we all can get out in this weather. Me, you, our wives, and the police. So, I suggest that until that day comes, you think of how you want to go about this." With that, he hung up.

I broke the hug, but not letting go of Christian completely. Mrs. O'rion hugged me, then Christian. "You two go to bed, it's late." I looked at her, confused. "I am going to sleep in Sabrina's room, right?" Christian stepped forward and said, "Like hell you are! You are not leaving my sight!" His mom smiled at us and hugged me again, a little longer and tighter this time. "I trust you both, you can sleep with him in his room if you want to." I looked back and forth between Christian's parents. "Thank you both so much for believing me and sticking up for me. I have never had that before." His dad gave me a sad smile and said, "You are safe now, Anna, get some sleep." We headed to Christian's room and he shut the door.

"You can wear one of my shirts to bed. I'm going to get a shower, you can get one after me if you want," he says, caressing my cheek. "Thank you, which shirt?" I asked. He walked to his closet and opened the door. "You pick. I can find Sabrina's shorts that she left here when she left for college." I nodded, not saying anything. Suddenly, I felt nervous, not knowing why. He walked to his bathroom that connected to his room and shut the door. I heard the shower turn on, so I grabbed a shirt to change into.

About ten minutes later, the shower turned off and a few minutes after that, he walked out into his room, wearing nothing but gym shorts. I was standing by his closet, wearing just his shirt, which hung off me like I was five years old. I turned my head to look at him and he stopped completely. *Damn, I really want to run my hands over his chest and shoulders.* I looked him up and down then rested my eyes on his chest and shoulders. *Damn. Guys should not be this pretty.* Looking nervous, he said, "Um, I can go find those shorts for you while you get in the shower. I set a towel out on the sink for you." I nodded and walked past him into the bathroom.

Standing in the shower, I let the hot water take over my senses. I should have been exhausted, the evening had been crazy, but all I could think about was sleeping next to Christian, feeling his body against me all night. My safety blanket. I was still a virgin, wanting to wait till marriage. But in that moment, all I could think of was being with him. I replayed what he told his dad about me and smiled. I was his life and I trusted him with mine. I was, for the first time, one hundred percent safe, as long as I was with him. I turned off the shower, dried off, and put on his shirt again.

I walked into his room and he had music on. "I always sleep with music on, but I can turn it off if you want me to," he said, still looking at his computer. "You can leave it on, that's fine with me," I tell him softly. He turned from his computer and looked me up and down. I shivered under his stare. He frowned. "Are you cold?" He still wasn't wearing a shirt. *Damn it, he looks so damn good.* I bit my lower lip and shook my head. He stood up. "You are shivering, Anna." He started walking towards me and I stood there, stuck like a deer in headlights. He wrapped his arms around me. My hands cautiously went up, spreading my fingers out over his chest. I traced his skin from his chest to his shoulders, memorizing every muscle and curve of his body. He hummed in pleasure. "You ready to lay down?" I nodded and he picked me up like I weighed nothing, but to him, I probably didn't. He set me on the bed and I slid over toward the inside wall so he could climb in.

We faced each other. "How long has he been hurting you, Anna?" He asked me softly. Tears welled up in my eyes. "Since I was about four years old," I answered him, not able to look him in the eyes. He let out a breath roughly. He lifted my head with his index finger under my chin. "Look at me, please, I need to see you," I looked into his eyes, feeling vulnerable. "Has he ever hit you because of me?" At that question, tears spilled from my eyes. "Yes," I told him. He shut his eyes tightly and exhaled again. "He will never touch you again, Anna," he said sternly then kissed me, soft and slow.

"Anna, I love you so much," he said, not taking his eyes off mine. "I love you with everything I am, Christian," I responded sincerely, "but I am also scared."

"Scared of what, baby?" He said, looking confused. I took a deep breath and answered him. "Scared of loving you too much, losing you. We are just kids to most people, but I can tell you with full confidence that I have never felt so safe and loved with anyone except with you. You are my safe place, Christian." I turned on my back, looking up at the ceiling, and he leaned over me. "You *are* safe. You are loved." He looked at me with his gorgeous eyes. "I am all yours and only yours, that will never change. They can say we do not know because we are just kids, but I know. I do not need anyone else's approval on this."

I needed him, wanted him in every way possible. "Christian? Can I ask you something?" I whispered nervously. "Of course, ask me anything. No judgment here at all." I bit my lower lip. "Where do you see this going with us? Like, in the long run?" He didn't flinch or even take a minute to think about what I asked. "I will love you forever, Anna. Until I die." I took in his facial features, memorizing them more than I already had. "Me too, Christian. I want all of you, forever." He grinned that half grin of his that drove me insane. "You have all of me for as long as you want me."

"I want you to have all of me," I told him, my voice clear and confident. It took him a minute to register what I was telling him. I felt his grip tighten on my waist. "Anna, are you sure?" It was my turn to smile at him. "Christian, I love you, I will always love you, for my entire life. If I have it my way, you will be my first and only." His beautiful blue eyes darken. "I will be your only."

# PIECE BY PIECE

"Earth to Anna!" Alex said, snapping her fingers in my face. I blinked. "What?" I said as I brought myself out of my fantasy and back to reality. "Tomorrow night's football game, we are going, right?" She asked me while looking at me like I had lost my mind. "Of course, we are going," Lisa chimed in. "She will not miss a chance to see Christian in those football pants." I rolled my eyes at her, but she was not wrong.

Lunch was almost over, so we headed to our lockers. "I'll see you all later," I told them and went off to get my books for my next class. "Anna?" I heard Christian's voice behind me and I froze. I turned around; he was standing a few feet from me, his hands in his pockets. I looked around to make sure Jack wasn't close. "Hey, uh, Christian, what's up?" My heart was close to exploding. I wanted to tell him everything, but I couldn't.

"You're planning on going to the game tomorrow night, right?" I shrugged. "I've thought about it," was all I could say, my nerves going haywire. He broke out in that grin that melted me and I could swear he could read everything I had been thinking to myself. "Well, I was thinking, if you wanted to, you could wear my jersey?" *Holy shit! Keep your mouth closed, Anna, do not let it hit the floor!*

"Really?" I asked, actually surprised he would even want me to. "Yeah, really. I asked you, didn't I?" That was his way of flirting, I knew it. I giggled and then nodded. "Sure, I would like to." Then we walked to his locker and he gave me the extra jersey he had in it. He held it out for me but when I grabbed it, he did not let go. "I was also thinking, maybe we could hang out before the game? At my house?" I wanted to cry. I wished I had the strength to tell him everything. "Sure, that would be fine. I have nothing else going on." He smirked. *Stay upright, Anna, don't let your knees fail you.*

"I will be driving the Chevelle," he told me. "I mean, you did promise me a ride in it." I teased him, but he turned serious. "I remember." I couldn't read his face. The bell rang. "I better head to class," I said as I took the jersey from him. "I can walk with you if you want," he offered and we went to class.

After school, I reached home and hid his jersey in my bag before stepping in. That night at dinner, I was in my own little world, not paying attention to anything going on around me. I kept fantasizing about being alone with Christian the next evening. My mom brought me out of my thoughts. "Anna, are you going to the game tomorrow?" She asked me. I shrugged like the game was no big deal when in reality, it was the highlight of my year. "I've thought about it. Alex and Lisa talked about staying after school and grabbing a bite to eat before the game and after practice," I answered her.

Bud chimed in. "Alex is a bad influence." I looked at him as innocently as I could. "Because she wants to grab dinner?" I asked him, my voice soft. He pointed his fork at me. "You know what I mean, don't play dumb with me." I shrugged again. "You may think that but I make my own choices, she doesn't make them for me." I focused on my dinner again. That clearly irritated him, but he let it slide. "What about after the game?" He asked me, eyeing me suspiciously. "Lisa wants me to crash with her, she has been getting a lot of crap lately and she is upset, so I want to help get her mind off things," I lied to him and it worked.

"Why don't you just beat the shit out of whoever is making her upset like you did with Stacy?" Bud said to me in a snarky, smug tone. He loved to bring up that fight and I hated him for it, among many other reasons. My mom cut in, saying "Please don't fight anymore, sweetheart."

"She would be defending someone," Bud said, "Just don't throw the first punch. Run your mouth like you do with me to get them to do it."

## PIECE BY PIECE

"Don't throw the first punch, only the last, got it," I said. "That's right!" He said, smiling at me. What I wouldn't give to throw the last fucking punch at you, I thought to myself. *Maybe someday.*

## CHAPTER 20

*Now*

We tuck the girls into bed and head out to the porch. Rafe grabs a couple of beers, handing me one. "Drink it, we need it," he says. I sigh, "You're right, this is getting insane." I take a long pull from mine then reach down to pet Bane, who is lying at my feet. *My sweet boy.*

"So, what do you want to do about this?" Rafe asks as he looks out over the yard and into the woods. I continue petting Bane, taking a few seconds to think. I take another pull from my beer before answering. "I have a plan, but you are not going to like it." He grins. "Since when do I like any of your 'plans'?" I laugh; he is right. "Touché."

He takes another drink and then stares at me. It's not fair for a man to look that good. I shake my head, dismissing the thought. *My deranged ex-stepbrother is stalking me and my family, and I am sitting here staring at my husband, wanting to take him to bed.*

"What?" he asks, looking confused. "Nothing, just thinking," I tell him, looking away to focus on the subject at hand. He sighs. "Does it involve you ending up in an orange jumpsuit?" he asks, only half-joking. I shrug. "The plan might, but I was actually thinking about no clothes at all." I wink at him. He leans in and gives me a kiss. "Let's discuss that plan of yours first," he grins, "the other can wait until after our discussion."

Long after Rafe falls asleep, I am still wide awake. I am too afraid to sleep. The nightmares are becoming more frequent. I go to the living room and turn on the TV, knowing I won't pay attention to what's on. About twenty minutes later, I walk out onto our deck, looking into the darkness. *My own darkness surrounds me, almost smothering me.* "God, make it stop!" I whisper into the night.

I feel hands grab my shirt and shoot me up into the air, but I see nothing or no one. I struggle, but I can't break free from the grip. We ascend so high that my house looks like a child's toy. The cold air hits me like a Mack truck. Then, I feel the warm breath of whatever has me up here. I start kicking and punching in that direction when I hear it—a laugh, pure evil. I become completely still. "I am going to kill you," I growl at it, "I am going to rip your fucking throat out with my bare hands!" I feel nothing but rage, yet I am calm. *It is the weirdest feeling.* I hear it growl, and the black figure I saw under the bed in my nightmare appears. This time, its wings, black and huge, are fanned out, keeping us in the air. It whispers in an evil voice, "You will lose." Then I recognize the voice. *Jack!* My blood feels like it's boiling. "Fuck you, coward!" The figure laughs and lets me go. I fall towards the ground so fast. I try to scream, but nothing comes out.

"Anna! Anna! Wake up!" Rafe yells at me. He is shaking me. I shoot straight up in our bed, gasping for air. His hands cup my face as he kneels in front of me. "Are you okay?" I look around the room, trying to collect myself. "Uh, yeah, sorry, just a bad dream," I say, attempting to make light of it. "That was more than a fucking bad dream, Anna," he tells me, his eyes full of concern. "I just want to lay back down, baby," I tell him as I collapse back onto the bed. He lies down beside me, and I curl up into him. Soon, Rafe was back asleep, but not me. I didn't want to get up, but I didn't want to sleep either. So, I laid there

# PIECE BY PIECE

in the dark, holding Rafe and thinking about the plan I have for Jack.

# CHAPTER 21

*Then*

I waited for Bud to leave for work. Then I put on Christian's jersey, tucking it into my 'Silver' brand flared jeans—the ones that looked painted on and that Bud hated. I looked at myself in the mirror, suddenly missing my long dark hair. *Oh well,* I shrugged at myself. I grabbed my book bag and headed for the door to leave. "Whose jersey is that?" I heard from behind me. *Fuck.* I turned and glared at him. "None of your fucking business, Jack. Who's wearing yours? Oh yeah, no one," I sneered at him. Before he could answer, I was in my car and going down the driveway. Once Jack figured it out, Bud would know. *I bet I will get a good beating for this one.* I smiled to myself, *"Worth it,"* I sang out loud, alone in my car.

## PIECE BY PIECE

The day dragged on and I was antsy for the last bell to ring. I had seen Christian a few times throughout the day, smiling at each other. He asked me at lunch if we were still on to hang out after school before the game. One part of me was so excited to be with him again, alone with him. The other part was worried and scared. *Do I confess what happened three years ago? What will happen if I do? What if Bud finds out I told him? Will he follow through on his threats?* I sat at my desk in the last class of the day, my thoughts a mess in my head. I was gnawing on my bottom lip. *Fuck, I need a drink,* I thought to myself as the final bell rang.

I practically ran to my locker to put my books away and to grab my jacket. Christian was nowhere to be found yet. My cell phone buzzed, indicating a text message. *'MEET ME AT MY CAR,'* Christian texted me. I smiled and headed for the door. Taking a right out the front of the school, I headed for the student parking lot. I searched for Jack's car just in case. I didn't need him seeing me getting into Christian's car. I didn't see it and I silently thanked God. It took me no time to find Christian's car. He was leaning against it, his arms folded across his chest. *Damn, what I wouldn't give to run up and jump into those arms of his.* I mentally told myself to calm down and not look so excited. He was talking with a few other football players when he noticed me. I suddenly felt extremely nervous and shy. He smiled at me with that damn smile of his. *It really should be against the law for him to have that smile and look that good.* The other guys followed his gaze to me and suddenly I felt extremely out of place. One of them, I knew for a fact, hated me and I wasn't sure why. That one rolled his eyes at me, his face not hiding his disgust. *What the fuck, dude? I don't even know you, just your reputation. Maybe that's why he hates me; he thinks he knows mine.* "See you guys later," he said to his teammates, and they walked away.

"Ready?" Christian asked me, looking me up and down. A shiver coursed through my body that I couldn't hide. "Are you cold, Anna?" he said, his brow furrowing. *No, you just give me chills,* I thought to myself. "No, I am good, and yes, I am ready." I gave him a smile, and we climbed into the car. I was almost afraid to touch this damn car. He fired it up, and we headed out of the parking lot and towards his house. Jack drove past us. *Fuck.* The windows were tinted; maybe he didn't see me. "Shit," I whispered out loud. "What?" Christian asked me as he looked in his rearview mirror. "Jack?" he asked me. I nodded. "Are you not supposed to be in my car or something?" he asked, sounding confused. *Or something,* I thought. *Do I tell him? No, he is driving, not a good idea to risk the car with his temper.* I sighed. "They think I am with Alex and Lisa. If he sees me with anyone else, he will run to his daddy and tell on me." I sneered, "He is such a little bitch, daddy's puppet." Christian laughed. "That is true. Want me to talk to him?" I laughed. "You mean, do I want you to threaten him?" He shrugged. "Same thing, isn't it?" I smirked. "No, but thank you. Alex will cover for me." He nodded, turning onto the main road that led to his house.

A few minutes went by, then he asked, "You scared?" I turned from the window and looked at him. "Of?" He smirked at me. *Asshole.* "Do you trust me?" he asked. *More than anyone I have ever met,* I thought to myself. "Yes," I said, confused. He looked back out the windshield. "Good." He then slammed on the gas, gunning it. The car took off, leaving my stomach back where we started. He switched gears so easily; it seemed like he had been doing it for longer than he had been actually driving. He eyed me every few seconds to gauge my reaction. *Is he testing me? For what? To see if I am really scared or if I really trust him?* I laughed. "That's it? That is all you got, huh?" I yelled over the sound of the engine, teasing him. He laughed and punched it again. I watched how he drove with ease. *Maybe he could teach me,* I thought to myself.

We made it to his house and he pulled the car into the garage. I noticed no other cars in the drive. As if reading my mind, he told me that his mom was at work and would head straight to the game after, and his dad was out of town. I nodded, my stomach turning with nervousness. *This will be interesting.* We headed inside, and he went straight to his room after we took our shoes off. *Do I follow him?* I stood in the doorway, debating what to do when I heard music from his computer. I walked to the door of his bedroom and stood in the entryway. "You can come in, you know," he said as he held his hand out to me. I didn't hesitate; I took his hand and let him pull me to him. He wrapped his arms around my waist. All I could do was look at him, trying to read his face.

"Do you still want me, Anna?" His question caught me off guard. *What do I tell him? That I have never stopped wanting him and never would? That every day without him kills me slowly?* I had learned that the truth is not always the best and gets you in trouble. This truth, if I told him, could ruin more than just my life. His tone in the question, the way he was looking at me, had an underlying meaning that I wasn't sure I understood. "Yes, Christian, I still want you," I whispered. He kissed me then, and everything disappeared but us. All the bad, the pain—it was all gone. The kiss deepened, and both our breathing grew heavy. The physical attraction to him was apparent to anyone who looked. The jersey came off, and he threw it to the floor. His shirt was next. *Those damn shoulders of his.* I ran my hands over them and down his arms. *I have my safe place back.* He picked me up and carried me to his bed, not once breaking our kiss.

His room was dark, making it hard to see anything. He was on top of me; his weight felt so damn good. His hips ground into mine, and I could feel his intentions. He kissed my neck, knowing that was the spot that got me every time. His hand found the button of my jeans. "As much as I love seeing you in these jeans, I would love to see them on my floor more," he said between kisses. *I wanted so badly for him to be my first and, honestly, if I had it my way, my only. I was robbed of that, and so was he. Even if he doesn't know that, he will never know.* He pulled my jeans off and kissed a trail from my neck to my stomach. *Fuck, he feels so good.* His weight was off me, and I wanted to cry. It was too dark to see anything, but I could hear him removing his clothes. Then I felt his weight again, the heat from his body on mine, and I thought I was going to lose my mind.

It was when I heard the unmistakable sound of the packaging tearing open that I froze. Suddenly, I was back to that night, in the dark, when I had no choice. My mind fought between panic and reasoning. *Christian would never hurt me in any way, I know this, but I would be lying if I said I wasn't scared.* I didn't know what to do, so I did nothing. He couldn't see the panic on my face with how dark it was. "Are you okay?" he asked me. *No, I am not.* "Yes," I told him. *How can I want this and him so bad, but at the same time be terrified?*

After, he got dressed and headed out, leaving me alone in the darkness of his room. *What the fuck?* I heard his mom's voice. *So much for her working until the game,* I thought to myself, but I was also excited to see her. *Oh my God, how long has she been home? Does she know what we just did?*

I walked into the kitchen, shyly. Christian was eating, acting like nothing had happened. He didn't even look at me. "Anna! What a pleasant surprise! How are you?" She beamed, pulling me in for a hug. She looked me over. "Oh, hunny, you need to eat something! You are way too skinny!" I laughed nervously. "I just look like that because Christian's jersey is huge on me." No need to tell her my diet was mostly Gatorade and vodka, with my workouts being a beating from Bud. *Real athlete I am.*

Christian finished eating without saying a word while I visited with his mom. "Ready?" he asked as he put his dishes in the sink. *Something is wrong, I can feel it. What did I do?* "Uh, yeah," I answered him, grabbing my coat. He kissed his mom goodbye, telling her he would see her at the game. She waved at me. Christian walked out to his car without looking at me, leaving me to hurry to catch up. *Something is definitely wrong.* His one step was three of mine, and at his pace, I was not keeping up without running. He was in the car and had it running by the time I climbed in. I put on my seatbelt, unable to shake the feeling that he was mad at me and I didn't know why. *If I ask him, I risk having to tell him why I can't be with him or why I was so nervous a little while ago. I can't tell him how much I think about him and only want him.* I stayed quiet instead.

The next Monday, I headed to class as usual. Apparently, Jack never saw me with Christian, because I was never questioned once about what I did Friday. As I walked into class and got to my seat, I heard a few snickers and giggles. That was normal, but for some reason, this time, I felt something was worse about it. I did as I had trained myself to do—ignored it and acted like nothing was happening.

Alex came in and sat by me. "Hey," I said, and she looked at me with sad eyes. "I am, um, guessing you haven't heard?" she whispered to me. I looked at her, confused, but before I could answer her, Trent shouted at me. He was the obnoxious guy in our class. He was popular, and I couldn't figure out why because he was a huge douchebag. "Well, well, Anna!" *Fuck, what does he want with me?* "You are not as wild as you let on!" *What?* "Fuck off, Trent," I said, looking through my school book, acting like I didn't give a fuck. He continued, "Come on! Here we all were thinking you're some sort of bad girl. When in reality, I hear..." He stopped to make sure he had an audience. "That a guy using his own hand is more fun than you!" He burst out laughing. "What are you talking about, dumbass?" I snapped at him. "Christian told everyone that having sex with a sex doll is more fun than you! That you just lay there and do nothing! He also said it was the worst sex he ever had in his life!" The whole class laughed except for me and Alex.

*He wouldn't say that. Christian would never hurt me like this.* But then how would the school know we had sex if he didn't? The pain from what he had done was worse than any beating I got from Bud—worse than all of them combined. The embarrassment pissed me off. *I really can't trust anyone.* I said the first thing that came to my mind, "Trent, think about it. If my reputation is what you say it is, then it can't be true. Maybe he is lying to hide the fact that I was actually bored and he wasn't good. He just ran his mouth before I could say anything." I grinned at him when I really wanted to cry. My remark hit where I wanted it to. Trent burst out laughing, and the class echoed a "Whoa." Trent said, "You're right, that does make more sense and it makes it even more hilarious!"

## PIECE BY PIECE

The teacher walked in then to start the class. I wanted to leave, to die, just fucking die. The one person I trusted with my life had hurt me. *Now what do I do?* He wouldn't believe me if I told him the truth anyway. And if he wouldn't believe that, then he definitely wouldn't believe me about Bud. *So did he just use me? Payback for breaking up with him? Now he got what he wanted and he is done with me. That would fit his reputation.* Just when I thought life couldn't be any worse.

After class, I went to my locker and got his jersey. I found him at his locker and wanted to cry and run. I tapped his arm because I wasn't standing on tiptoe to reach his shoulders. He turned around, his expression one of irritation. I slammed the jersey into his chest. "My mom washed it," I said, holding back tears. "You have lived up to your reputation, O'Rion. Congratulations!" I could feel the tears fill my eyes. I turned to leave, and he called out to me, "Anna! Wait!" I turned back to him. "No, Christian! You have no clue! No fucking clue!" I yelled as the tears rolled down my cheeks. "I am disappointed in myself for believing your bullshit!"

"You left me, Anna, not the other way around," he said softly. I nodded. "Yes, Christian, yes I did." I walked away from him and headed straight to my car. *Fuck today!* Grabbing the

## PIECE BY PIECE

Gatorade bottle, I slammed its contents and took off out of the parking lot, bawling my eyes out.

## CHAPTER 22

*Now*

A few days have gone by and I think Jack is just laying low. There has been no sign of him. I call the facility Josie is at. "Hey, Mrs. Garrison, the doctor was hoping to speak with you," the receptionist tells me. "Okay, thank you. Can you put me through, please?" I ask, already feeling the migraine. As the line switches, I light a cigarette. The line rings twice before he answers, "Dr. Hendrix speaking." I blow the smoke out, "Dr. Hendrix, this is Anna Garrison, I am Josie's sister and guardian." There was a pause and I could hear papers being shuffled around. "Yes, Mrs. Garrison, thank you for calling and making time to speak with me," he says. *Get on with it, Doc,* I think, wanting this conversation to be over. "Of course, anything for Josie," I tell him.

"I have had a few sessions with Josie so far, but I did want to talk to you about a few things she mentioned," he tells me.

"Sure, Doc, go ahead," I say, sounding irritated and not meaning to. Even if I was. He clears his throat, "Well, Josie holds you in such high regard, she loves you very much." I tell him I know, wanting him to get to the point already.

"Why, at Josie's age, are you her guardian and not her mom?" He asks. I laugh, "Well, how much time have you got for me to answer that one, Doc?"

Before I know it, our conversation is an hour and a half deep. "Mrs. Garrison, you're a psychiatrist, you must know that Josie needs to be able to be her own guardian, to learn to be independent and take care of herself, without outside help. She cannot rely on you forever."

I am instantly mad and defensive, "Actually, Doc, she can."

He sighs, "You know what I mean." His voice stern, like I am some patient.

"What you two have been through, is traumatizing, to say the least. You both have grown from it in two completely different ways."

"Yup, your point?" I say, not hiding my irritation.

"So, she hasn't really gotten over it, grown from it, faced it the way she should. She doesn't want to be fixed. In her mind, if she is fixed then you have no reason to have a relationship of any kind with her, and she can't handle that."

"That is bullshit, Doc."

"Yes, you and I know that, but she doesn't."

I sigh. *He is right. Damn it.* "So what do I need to do?" I ask him as I light another cigarette. *Chain smoking Anna? Yeah, that'll help.*

"Would you be able to come here and have a face-to-face visit?" He asks. His voice always professional.

"I would but, I have some issues of my own I need to handle here at home," I tell him as I take another pull from my cigarette.

"Jack?" He says. He didn't even try to ease into that. I am instantly tense and on edge. My anger building at just the sound of his name.

"Yeah, but how do you know?" I spit out already knowing the answer.

"Josie told me," He says, confirming what I already know, "Plus, he calls her daily." Now I am shaking and looking for something to throw or punch or both. That piece of shit! I try to calm down as I ask him why, but my tone gives me away.

I hear him take a deep breath about to tell me something significant, "Honestly, we do not know because she refuses his calls. When anyone here tells him that, we end up having to hang up on him because he is yelling and threatening everyone, including her." I give a low chuckle. That sounds like Jack alright.

"Josie goes into a full meltdown every day because of it and we are having to give her daily medications to calm her down." He tells me, sounding sad. I cuss and I really don't give a shit if he hears or cares.

"Do not ask her anymore ok? Do not tell her he even called. From now on, if he does call, you tell him that it was requested by her guardian that he not speak to her at all."

"What do we tell him when he asks who that is?"

"He can figure that out himself."

"OK then, I will put it in her chart. I do think a face-to-face would be beneficial to her and you."

"Understood, but I have one more question before I agree."

"What is that?"

"Do you allow dogs into your facility?"

After we hang up, I go back in the house to see Rafe and our girls sitting on the couch with popcorn. They are all engrossed in "The Croods" movie, Rafe included. He sees me first and can tell by the look on my face that we need to talk. He gets off the couch, looking at the girls, "Give me a minute girls, I will be back, I got to talk to mom. Do not eat all the popcorn." He says teasingly.

Jessie looks at him with the sweetest smile, "No promises Daddy." I laugh and shake my head. She then grabs a handful of popcorn, shoving it in her mouth while staring right at Rafe.

He rumples her head, "Little Turd."

## PIECE BY PIECE

"I am not poop Daddy!"

We walk into our room and Rafe shuts the door so that the girls cannot hear us. "What is it? I saw you on the phone, chain-smoking."

"Bane and I have to go to Seattle. There are some things with Josie I need to handle in person."

"OK, but what about Jack?"

I sigh, "Turns out he has been trying to call her daily and then harassing and threatening the staff when she refuses. I do not think she knows I am her guardian, but it wouldn't take much for him to figure that out."

Rafe nods, folding his arms across his chest, "So if you go, then he will for sure find out."

"That is what I am hoping."

Rafe runs his hands down his face, squeezing his eyes shut, then open a few times. "Why? Why, Anna, do you hope that? You know that will set him off."

"Exactly."

"You want to set him off? We have no clue what he will do!"

"Doesn't matter what he does, Rafe. I will be ready when he does."

"Alone! In Seattle!"

I shrug, I get why he is getting upset, but better to deal with him there than here with my kids around. I grab his hand, interlocking our fingers and wrapping the other around his neck, "While I am gone, you and the girls go stay with your parents."

"I don't need protection, Anna. I will go with you."

I kiss him, "No, you don't need protecting and I need you here with our girls. Help your dad protect them, at his age he will need it, especially with Jessie." I smile at him.

"I am going to tell him you said that." He sighs, "When are you leaving?"

"Tomorrow with Bane."

Rafe laughs, "Of course with Bane."

## CHAPTER 23

*Then*

Junior year was over. Christian had graduated and moved to South Carolina for college. Jack took off to Washington State to, as he put it, "Find Himself." I spent that summer and all of senior year in a bottle. With Christian out of state, Bud had, for the most part, backed off. We still had our moments, obviously.

I was not sure what was worse: Christian being at school where I had to see him every day, knowing I would never be with him again, or Christian not being around at all. Both made me feel empty. Nothing I did, not even the alcohol, got him out of my damn head.

## PIECE BY PIECE

Any guy who showed me the slightest bit of attention I compared to him. They all fell short. No one would ever make me feel the way Christian did in the beginning.

My depression, panic attacks, and anger were out of control, even for me. I couldn't stop though. It was my fault for what happened. My fault that he hurt me the way he did. If I had just told him the truth, then we would still be together. He would never know or understand I was protecting him. Bud had ruined my life, and I would not let him ruin Christian's.

Christian also did not know what had happened to me that night a few years ago. Why I froze with him that night before the game. I could not tell him why I was so scared, even with him. If he had known everything, this wouldn't be happening. He wouldn't have hurt me. He loved me, I knew he did.

This daily war in my head about him made my hate for Bud and Jack worse with each passing day. I didn't just hate them for what I had to do to protect Christian, but for what they were doing to Josie. She was eleven now and struggling in school in every way, which only caused more issues between her and Bud.

PIECE BY PIECE

My reputation in school and around town had turned to something else. Now when people saw me, they didn't think 'what a whore,' they thought about my anger and outbursts. Especially where Josie was concerned. They looked at her sideways and I was in their face, and it was almost always violent. *She gets hurt enough at home. I will be damned if it happens outside the house.*

I had given up long ago about trying to report Bud. Every time I tried, I was labeled 'dramatic' and 'a liar.' No one paid any attention to my actions and saw them for what they were, a cry for help. I became my own hero, my own protector. I got really good at sarcasm and shooting off my mouth to hide the pain. I did this a lot. Mostly towards my mom and Bud.

*How could she let him do this to her kids, to me? How could she lie for him when he got questioned by any adult? Did she not see it? Of course she did, well maybe not all of it, but most of it. She definitely did not know about the truth with Christian.*

I graduated and spent the summer working and partying, trying to figure out what I wanted to do with my life. I knew I at least wanted to get as far away from Bud as possible, but that would mean leaving Josie and my mom here with him alone. *I can't do that. I have to stay close for them. I have to be able to protect them.*

Halfway through that summer after graduation, I was out driving around after getting off work and waiting for Alex to meet up with me. My cell phone beeped, alerting me I had gotten a text, but I didn't recognize the number.

'Hey, Anna. How are you? It has been a long time!'

I pulled into the local gas station to answer and get some cigarettes. 'Who is this?' I texted back as I went into the store.

As I headed back to my car, lighting a cigarette, my phone beeped again. 'Christian.'

I almost choked on the inhale of smoke from the cigarette. *Someone is fucking with me, I know it.*

'Right, good one Fuck Tard,' I replied back and decided to head out to my favorite spot at the river. Alex would know where I was if she couldn't find me in town.

I started my walk down the trail through the woods to my spot when my phone rang. It was an incoming call. Maybe Alex, so I did not check to see who it was, I just answered it. "Hey bitch, where are you?" I said, laughing to myself. We were the only ones who could call each other that without risking a beat down. I loved her like she was my sister.

"Um, Anna? Hey, this really is Christian."

I stopped dead in the middle of the trail, my heart leaping out of my chest. *Holy fuck that really is his voice, I would know it anywhere.* "Christian?" I asked because I was a dumbass.

He laughed. *Fuck how I have missed his laugh.* "Yeah, duh, it is really me. Who did you think it was?"

"Um, no one. But how? Why? Fuck, sorry. I mean what's up Christian?" I rolled my eyes, *dumbass,* I thought to myself.

"I got your number from Dom. I wanted to check on you, make sure you are ok."

*Damn it, Dom, I will kick his ass later or give him a big kiss, I don't know which yet.* "I am fine, great, actually," I lied to him.

There was a slight pause. "Are you though?" He asked as if he knew I was full of shit, which I was.

"What did you really want, Christian?" I said sounding irritated.

"Um, honestly, I was thinking about how you'd feel if I asked you to come out here to see me, maybe."

I closed my eyes and did a little happy dance and punched the air. Then I quickly calmed back down, "Where is here, Christian?" I asked, playing dumb. "Are you home or something?" *If he is, I will lose my shit!*

"No, you come out here to South Carolina," he said almost nervously.

I lit another cigarette, "Why would I want to do that?"

"Because, Anna, I want to see you. I miss seeing you, honestly."

*If my heart had wings, it would be flying.* "Yeah? Well, that makes two of us."

My phone beeped, indicating an incoming call. I checked to see who it was, my mom. "Hey, my mom is calling, you can text me if you want."

"I will. Good night, Anna."

"Night, Christian."

I answered my mom, trying to hide my excitement, "Hey mom."

"Hey hun, what are you up to?"

"I was waiting on Alex; we are supposed to hang out soon. Why? What's up?"

"Nothing, I was just in town and ran into Christian's mom."

"Oh yeah? How is she?"

"Fine. She said Christian wanted your number and I wanted to check with you before I gave it out. I wasn't sure how you would feel about that."

I grinned, biting my bottom lip. "I appreciate that, Mom, but Dom already gave it to him, I was just on the phone with him actually."

"Oh! How was that? Everything okay?"

"Yeah, Mom, he actually wanted to see if I would come out to see him in South Carolina for a few days."

Silence. "Mom?"

## PIECE BY PIECE

"Uh, yeah, I'm here. Do you want to go?"

"Yeah, Mom, I think I do."

"Well, you're an adult now, so if you want to, that's fine with me, but I just don't want you getting your hopes up and then hurt."

"I get that, Mom. But I have a favor to ask."

"Yeah, baby?"

"Can we keep this between us till I am ready to announce it? That would mean..."

She laughed, "It would mean not to say anything to Bud. Yes, it can be our secret, for now."

"Thank you, Mom."

We hung up and I thought how ironic it was that she didn't want me hurt by Christian, but she allowed Bud to. I started walking again and my phone beeped. *Damn people, leave me alone,* I thought to myself. 'Can't wait till you are here. Let me know when and I will pick you up at the airport.' Another beep sounded as another message came in. 'Where are you, Bitch! I need a drink!' I smiled. *Maybe things were going to get better.*

## CHAPTER 24

*Now*

Bane and I arrive in Seattle the next morning. Getting a rental car and hotel on such short notice is exhausting. I decide to take a nap at the hotel before facing Josie. *Maybe I just need a drink,* I think to myself. *No, I can't do that.*

Three hours later, after a quick nap, a hot shower, and some food, Bane and I head out to the facility. True to its reputation, Seattle is nothing but rain. I hate cities, especially big ones. With the rain and busy traffic, my anxiety is through the roof, and my nerves are shot by the time we arrive. It only took me thirty minutes to go ten miles or so.

I find a parking spot and get out, leashing Bane. He doesn't need one, but it was a requirement to bring him. We head inside and go to the front desk. An older, plump woman who would classify as the stereotypical grandma greets me.

"Well hello! How can I help you?" She looks at Bane and beams, "I mean, how can I help you two?"

I politely smile back. "I am here to see Dr. Hendrix."

"Certainly! Can I get your name, please?"

"Dr. Anna Garrison."

Her face goes white as she looks at me with big round eyes. "Josie's sister?"

*Oh shit,* I think. "Uh, yes ma'am."

"Um, okay, um, let me, uh, let me call him." She stammers as she picks up the desk phone, dialing a few numbers. She announces to him that I am here and then looks up at me. "No sir, I haven't." She practically whispers into the phone. I wonder if he heard her because I barely could. She gives me a sad smile. "Yes sir, I will let her know." She hangs up the phone. "Dr. Hendrix will be with you shortly. He, uh, wanted me to inform you that Jack has already called three times this morning."

I don't even flinch. "And?" I ask, needing more information than that.

"And he is demanding to speak to Josie and won't stop calling till he does. He says he wants to know who is in control over her."

"Did you tell him?"

"Oh no, ma'am, never! He did threaten to come here if we don't let him talk to her."

*Of course he did,* I think to myself, holding my composure.

"What would you like us to do, Dr. Garrison?"

"Doctor Anna, I presume?" I hear from behind me, cutting our conversation off.

I turn to see a man in his mid-seventies. With a full head of white hair, he is remarkably tall and fit for his age. He reminds me of Sam Elliott. "And this," he says as he bends down to be at the same level as Bane, "must be the famous Bane." Bane is loving all this attention.

I clear my throat because I am nervous. "You must be Doctor Hendrix?"

Still giving his full attention to Bane by scratching his ears, he replies, "The one and only!" Then he stands to shake my hand. He gestures towards the hall. "Shall we? My office is this way." I nod, then quickly turn to the lady at the desk. "If he calls again, place him on hold and let me speak with him."

"Yes, ma'am," she says quietly.

Doctor Hendrix gives a low whistle. "That should be interesting, of that I have no doubt."

I say nothing and head the way he pointed. His office reminds me of an old man's smoking lounge. Dark leather chairs, and a huge cherry wood desk. There are matching bookshelves behind it, full of various books. No pictures, no art. The floors are dark wood planks that look real and not vinyl. An area rug with a woodland theme covers most of the floor.

He takes a seat in his high-back chair behind his desk that matches the ones he has for visitors to sit across from him. I take a seat as I look around, Bane laying down at the side of my chair.

"Is this where you have your sessions?" I ask.

"No, it is normally too intimidating for visitors, let alone patients," he says with a smile.

# PIECE BY PIECE

"I like it."

"Thank you."

"So, where is my sister?" I ask, wanting to get this over with and get back home to Rafe and my girls.

"She will be here shortly. She likes this room as well. I have not told her that you were coming."

I nod, having figured as much, but I ask why anyway.

"Her anxiety is crippling, Doctor Garrison." He smiles. "Anna. You are the only person she trusts, but she still will worry herself into sickness. I wanted to avoid that."

"So, surprising her will avoid that?" I ask, confused.

He gives me a weak grin. "She will not have the time to sit and dwell on it."

"That is fair."

"Before she gets here, Anna, I have to ask, why are you still taking responsibility for her? She is an adult now."

I take a few seconds to gather myself and come down off the defensive ledge I am instantly on. *Trying to answer without coming across as defensive or angry?* My face must give me away. I look down at Bane to center myself.

"Anna, trauma like the one you both faced can manifest in many forms. PTSD is an ugly thing. Josie seeks attention through suicidal risks, mostly by taking pills, but even though it's bad, she needs that attention. Then there is you," he says with a big sigh, "you're the fighter, in any way you can fight. You feel you have to prove yourself, to prove you're not weak. You are the strong one everyone can go to and rely on, while you only rely on yourself. You trust no one. To you, everyone has a hidden agenda."

I hold my hand up to silence him. "Look, I get it, but I have learned to harness my anger. I found God when for the longest time I didn't even think he existed. In doing that, he gave me my husband and my girls. He gave me Bane."

His gaze shifts to Bane, who is asleep on the floor now. "You rely on your dog a lot," he says as a statement, not a question. Instinctively, I reach for Bane, running my hands down his back. "He is your safety?"

I nod. *Just like Christian used to be.* I think to myself. *What the fuck? Where did that come from?*

# PIECE BY PIECE

"Back to my original question, Anna. Why?"

"I have looked after Jo-jo, Josie, since she was born. I have protected her to the best of my ability. That will never change, ever."

"And your husband? He understands? He knows everything?"

I nod. "He is an amazing man and never questions what I do for Josie."

He interlocks his fingers, resting his elbows on the arms of his chair. "Do you have any intention of letting her fight her own battles? The ones, for instance, you can't fight for her, like the ones in her head?"

"I would even fight those for her if I could," I tell him, shifting in my seat. "If I let her try, I could lose her. She has come so close, but the last time was the closest, and I won't risk that."

He leans forward now, resting his arms on the desk. "Anna, I do not think she did this to herself this time."

I cock my head, confused. "What do you mean? It was a suicide attempt, like the others, right?"

"I think someone tried to kill her and make it look that way."

I am out of my chair so fast I startle Bane. "What the fuck, Doc! Why couldn't you start with that?" I yell at him as I start to pace his office, Bane watching me, trying to gauge what I am feeling.

"Calm down, please, Anna. This is just an assumption I have. I cannot prove it to be true," his voice even and calm. I know that tone; I use it with my own patients.

I stop my pacing and face him. "Jack?" I ask, balling my fists at my sides. He nods.

"How and why would he do that? What would that benefit him?" I ask as I fall back into the chair. I crack my knuckles, then pet Bane to let him know I am okay.

"I think that is why he calls daily like he does and demands to speak with her. He is afraid she will remember."

"Remember?"

"Anna, when Josie was found unconscious by an unknown person, they said she hit her head as she overdosed and fell. The call came from her phone, in her apartment where it was found by her. When asked who the caller was, they hung up. The voice was male. There were no witnesses who saw or heard anything. That is why I think it was Jack, I just can't prove it."

"I can prove it was him."

"How?"

# CHAPTER 25

*Then*

I booked my flight two weeks after Christian first called me because I honestly could not afford next-day tickets. Every day felt like it was dragging on. The weekend before I left, to kill time, I cleaned my car, blaring Linkin Park from it. I wasn't paying attention at all, so focused on what I was doing and fantasizing about what it would be like to be with Christian again. I spun around to grab the vacuum that was behind me and ran right into Bud. He looked pissed.

I also noticed Jack hovering behind his own car, eavesdropping. *Fucking minion.* I turned off the music and turned back to Bud, "Hey Bud, sorry, I didn't see you there."

"Did you plan on telling me you were fucking going to see Christian?"

I cocked my head, pretending to be confused, "Weird, I didn't know I needed your permission since I paid for it myself."

I saw the red creep up his face, the veins in his head and neck throbbing as they stuck out. He gritted his teeth, "You live in my fucking house!" He yelled at me through clenched teeth. I swear I made him do that so much, it was a wonder his teeth hadn't broken.

"Truth, Bud, but I am eighteen now and I paid for my own flight and I pay rent, so you're really like a landlord. Last time I checked, I did not sign a lease agreement that states I was to tell you anything." I smirked at him. I flipped off Jack for good measure. *Fuck them both. They can't hurt us now.*

"I need to finish my car," I said as I tried to go around him. He grabbed my arm, tight enough to leave a bruise, and he slammed me into my car.

"You smart-ass little slut! I ought to..."

"Ought to what, Bud? Hit me? Beat my ass? I fucking dare you! Then I can go show Christian what you have done to me my whole life! Tell him the truth! Then you and your fucking minion," I said, pointing to Jack, "are done!"

Bud laughed, "What is that little spoiled man whore going to do? Fight me?"

I shrugged, "That would be cool to see."

His face went darker, if that was even possible, "Keep it up, girl, and…"

"I know, I know," I said, rolling my eyes, "you will whoop my ass. Well, go ahead! The only reason you even have a problem with Christian is because you both," I said, pointing back at Jack, "are scared of him! You were scared of him when he was sixteen! That's why you did what you did!"

His fists balled up at his sides. "Why the fuck would I be scared of a kid with no future but a criminal one?"

"Honestly, Bud, you make it so obvious. You're scared because you know that if he is in my life, then you have no control over me and that's what this is all about—control. As long as Christian is with me, you can't do anything to me because he would stop you. You hate the fact that you can't control or break me, especially if he's involved."

He laughed now, looking past me to the barn. "You think you are so smart. Got me all figured out, huh? You going to be a therapist, girly? No, you will be his whore forever. His plaything he only needs to play with once in a while. And when he is done with you? He will discard you worse than your own dad did. Who would want you then, huh? A woman beaten, living in a rundown trailer with ten kids from ten different daddies, living off the government. All the while, Christian will find him someone new, someone worth a shit. You won't even cross his mind. But you did break, Anna. You broke when I made you choose. You break every day," he said, grinning at me. Jack, behind him now, laughed.

"Aww, Bud, it's sad you think you have that much power over me. Aren't you still too young to lose your mind?"

"Just wait and see. You must think I'm a dumbass."

I nodded happily at him. He snorted, "Okay, girly." He walked away, and I wriggled my fingers at Jack. *Fucking idiots.*

Today is the day! I packed for my trip, and to say I was giddy and ecstatic would be an understatement. To be honest, I was scared as hell too. I planned to tell Christian everything, every detail from the beginning. How I was forced to make a choice that would forever alter our lives, the beatings, how I felt about him and always have, all of it. *I wonder how he will react to that information,* I thought to myself. *Will he be upset with me? Will he tell me to stay with him and never go back? Would he feel the same way and want to get married? Whoa, Anna!* I thought to myself. *Slow down. I never planned to get married ever. But he is my safe place.*

"You ready, hun?" my mom asked as she stood in the doorway to my room.

"Yes!" I practically sang as I grabbed my bag and headed for the car. Bud was standing on their deck, watching and looking pissed. He hadn't said much since the fight last weekend, and I was okay with that. *Bye, Fucker!* I said in my head as I waved and grinned at him. Two hours later, I was on the plane. I tried to relax, but it was no use. I attempted to read the book I brought, do a Sudoku puzzle, and even watch a movie, but nothing helped to ease my growing anticipation and anxiety.

When the plane landed and the approval to get off was announced, I was like a kid on a school bus, up and in front of the line so I could be the first one off. I turned on my phone and texted Christian. 'Landed. Meet you at baggage claim?' I hit send, then called my mom. She answered on the first ring, "Anna! You made it there safely?"

"Just got off the plane, Mom, heading to baggage claim to meet Christian," I told her, trying not to run there as I talked.

"Okay, baby, text me when you are with him. I worry about you being alone so far away."

I rolled my eyes. "I gotta go, Mom! Love you!"

"Love you."

We hung up, and a message from Christian was waiting. 'Can you find your way? I am here, waiting.' The butterflies in my stomach were going like it was a race to win. I found the escalator that goes down to baggage claim.

I barely got on and my phone rang. "Hello?"

"You are gorgeous, you know that?" His voice was like smooth whiskey warming my whole body while also giving me chills.

I giggled. "You're dumb. Where are you?" I asked, looking around. "There are too many people to see anything!"

He laughed, *fuck how I have missed his laugh.* "When you step off, turn left."

"You can see me?"

"Duh, why do you think I asked you if you knew how gorgeous you are?"

I stepped off and turned left, standing on my tiptoes to see, not that it did any good. Everyone was taller than me. "Where are you? I can't see you!"

"That's because you are short."

"Shut up and be nice!" I giggled. *I never giggle unless it involves Christian.*

"Do you see me now?" His voice had changed, now husky and wickedly lower. "Because I see you, and you are beautiful."

Just like a movie, the crowd seemed to part so I had a direct line of sight to where he was waiting. He was about twenty feet away. His smile was devastating. He was sexy and gorgeous, just like I remembered him being, even more so now. I was standing still, phone still to my ear.

"Come here, Anna,' he said as he hung up and held out his arms for me.

I bolted from where I stood, in a dead run, and launched myself into his arms. I held him tight, convincing myself I was dreaming. His arms surrounded me, and I was safe again. He was so damn strong it was addicting. He laughed, "Anna, I can't breathe."

I reluctantly let him go, "Sorry, I'm just excited."

He put his arms around me, holding my waist, and pulled me against him, "Me too." Then he kissed me, and not just a peck. His hands cupped my cheeks, and he gave me one of those deep, passionate kisses I had been dreaming about for as long as I could remember. He pulled back as we tried to catch our breath. He gave me another squeeze, "Let's get your bag and get out of here." His blue eyes hinted at what he wanted.

I gave him another kiss. "Okay." *I would follow him to hell if it meant being with him.*

# CHAPTER 26

"Anna? You're here," Josie says, looking shocked.

"Yeah, my Jo-jo. I've missed you and wanted to see you."

She runs into my arms, hugging me like I'm her lifeline. She looks terrible, and I want to cry. She drops down to love on Bane, who is wagging his cropped tail so hard his back end is shaking too. "You brought this sweet boy too!"

"Where I go, he goes too."

Dr. Hendrix clears his throat, interrupting our reunion. "Josie, your sister and I were just going over your history and how you ended up here."

## PIECE BY PIECE

Josie looks back and forth between us, her eyes filled with tears that want to fall, and my heart breaks. "Did you tell him everything?" she asks me quietly, her voice breaking.

I nod. "Yeah, Jo-jo, I did. We need to get a hold on this; you need to get a hold on this."

Fear takes over her face. "You are mad at me," her voice panicked.

I shake my head. "No, not at all, Jo-jo, I promise. I just can't protect you from yourself; you need to face this and beat it."

"I am not like Anna. I am not that strong."

I reach for Bane to relax me. *I am not as strong as you think. I still fight with myself every day. You need to fight yourself as well.*

We all sit in the chairs in his office, Bane again laying at my side. *Within my reach, good.* "Josie, can you tell Anna, in your own words, what happened with this last episode?"

Josie takes a deep breath and nods. She looks at me, her eyes pleading, "Let me finish before you say anything, Anna, please."

## PIECE BY PIECE

"I promise, Jo-jo," I vow as I hold back the tears, anxiety, and anger.

I can literally see her relax. Taking another deep breath, she starts to talk. "You know that Jack had been calling me, asking me questions. I told you that."

I nod, not saying anything like I promised her.

"Well, a few days before, he called me saying he wanted to come visit me. He didn't even bring you up at all. He said he wanted to 'clear the air' and to do it in person. I was hesitant at first, but it was a few days before my dad's, um, passing. I felt bad, so I invited him to my apartment."

The look on my face must have been enough because she held up a hand, "Wait, you promised."

*Damn it all, I did.* I nod at her to continue.

"He came over and I cooked supper for him. He was so talkative and positive. It was so unlike him, but I thought he was serious about fixing things. We had a few beers that he brought, and he asked if he could crash on the couch. Since he had been drinking, I let him stay so he wouldn't get in trouble when he left. I told him goodnight and headed for my room. The next thing I know, I am in the hospital and don't know why."

*I know why,* I think, trying to rein in my anger. I wait for her to keep going, but that was it. They both look at me. I take a few seconds to recover from the information she gave me and then turn to Dr. Hendrix, "I do not hide things from Josie, even if I think it is better she not know. I won't lie or hide things from her. Do you understand?"

He nods his understanding, and I turn to Josie. I take a breath and exhale before I begin, "Jo-jo, you need to know that Jack has been calling here daily, sometimes more than once, demanding to speak with you." She looks confused, "I thought the calls had stopped; I don't even know how he knew which facility I was at." *Good question,* I say to myself. "I don't either, Josie, but he is the one who did this to you. It was not a suicide like they think. Jack tried to kill you and make it look like a suicide. Now he is trying to find out what you remember about that night and if you told anyone."

She stares at me as if I have lost my mind. "Why?" she asks in an innocent voice like she had when she was a kid. The scared girl, she is showing through. "Josie, he has also been harassing and stalking me, Rafe, and the girls. He tried to get Dee to go with him to her school the other day." She covers her face, bursting into tears, "Oh my God."

"My guess is, he talked you into letting him into the apartment, drugged you with the beer he brought, tried to kill you, and cover it up. Then he went through your apartment, looking for any information on me. It is me he wants, Josie."

A knock at the door interrupts us, and the receptionist walks in, her face scared. "Sir, he has called again, he is on hold."

"Jack?" Josie asks, and she nods.

Dr. Hendrix looks at me. "What do you want to do?"

I look at Josie. "I will take that call."

"Are you sure?" the receptionist asks me, and I nod.

"Put him through to my office, please," Dr. Hendrix tells her. She nods and shuts the door. I can hear her footsteps as she goes back to her desk.

"Josie, why don't you..."

"No, she needs to be here," I tell Dr. Hendrix. He nods as the phone rings.

## PIECE BY PIECE

I look at Josie. "Jo-jo, I need you to stay quiet for me, okay?" She nods in agreement.

Dr. Hendrix answers the phone. "Dr. Hendrix speaking, how can I help you?"

He doesn't even put Jack on speakerphone, and I can hear him clearly as if he were standing in the room. "I want to talk to my fucking sister!" I hear Jack yell at the doctor.

His tone and vulgarity don't faze Dr. Hendrix at all. "I am sorry, sir, her guardian has requested she not take any calls from anyone and focus on getting better. So, I can't allow that."

"She is a grown-ass fucking woman! Who would make those kinds of rules for a grown fucking woman?" His tone and volume not changing at all.

"Well, it just so happens her guardian is sitting right here if you would like to ask them yourself?"

Silence. A few seconds pass before Dr. Hendrix asks if he is still there. "Yes, put them on." Jack finally answers.

I take the phone, saying a silent prayer that the shaking I am doing does not come through my voice and for God to give me the strength to handle this calmly. "This is Dr. Anna Garrison, can I help you?" Josie snorts and covers her mouth to hide the laugh. I pin her with a glare, and she mouths, 'sorry.'

"You fucking cunt!" Jack spits out.

"Aww now, Jack, no need for all that."

"Let me talk to her right fucking now!" he demands.

"Tsk, tsk. I cannot do that, Jack. You see, we have reason to believe that someone tried to kill Josie and pass it off as a suicide. So until I nail this guy, or gal, she won't be talking to anyone."

His voice gets lower. "She doesn't remember anyone who would want to do that to her?"

*Dumbass,* I think. "No, but I am willing to bet my own life I know who did."

He laughs. "You would gamble your own life on it?"

"Oh, Jack, I have done it before and I am still here to do it again. Or have you forgotten already?" I tell him in such a serious tone that even Dr. Hendrix's eyes get big.

"You will fucking pay for this!" Jack growls at me.

"I can't wait to pay that bill, Jack."

The line goes dead, and I hang up the phone. I stand up. "I have got to get back home, baby girl."

Josie panics. "Anna! He will kill you!"

I hug her. "You of all people should know better than that."

I shake Dr. Hendrix's hand. "Doc, he won't be calling here anymore. Please note this for legal reasons if any issues arise. Every call, threat, anything."

"We already have a file started," he tells me, grinning.

I turn back to Josie. "I want you here, in this place, till this is over. Spend this time helping yourself to get healthy and strong. The next time you have to face and fight your demons, I want you to do it alone. You are strong enough, Jo-jo."

She sobs and hugs me. "I love you, Anna."

I return the hug. "I love you too, my Jo-jo."

I call Bane, and we head home. *Now the fun starts.*

## CHAPTER 27

*Then*

The first few days with Christian had been heaven. We were pretty much glued to each other the entire time. He introduced me to his best friend and his girlfriend. I liked them; they were very nice and accepting, with no hint of judgment from either of them. I needed to tell him the truth about everything, but I was afraid to do it and ruin how things were going. *I will tell him tonight,* I decided.

"You're quiet," Janet said, interrupting my thoughts. She was Mason's girlfriend, who was Christian's best friend. She had invited me to spend the day with her at the beach since Mason and Christian had work.

I grinned shyly. "Just thinking about how beautiful it is here." I looked out at the ocean. I wasn't really a fan of the ocean, but if Christian was here, then I loved it.

"It is. I keep telling Mason that I want to have our wedding here since this is where we met."

"You guys are engaged?"

She laughed. "Not officially, but we do talk about it. Maybe after college."

"How long have you two been together?"

"Almost a year now," she told me, and she was glowing. Her love for him was unmistakable. She changed the topic to me. "You and Christian dated in high school, right?"

I nodded. "Yeah, off and on, kind of."

"What happened, if you don't mind me asking," her eyes burning holes into me, or at least that's how it felt.

I shrugged. "Young and dumb," I said, trying to play it off.

"You are still in love with him," she said. It was a statement, an observation, not a question.

No point in lying to her. "Yes, I am." I stared back at the waves, trying to hide my embarrassment. I hadn't even told Christian I still loved him, and here I was telling a complete stranger.

"That is so good! I like you way better than the other girl! For him mostly, but for us too. The other one was a snotty bitch, always acted like she was better than us," she said, shuddering.

"Other girl?" I asked. *What other girl?*

"She claimed she was his high school sweetheart. She was here about a week, same as you. I honestly think he is way too good for her. She was bossy and talked about herself the whole time," she said, rolling her eyes.

*Brittany.* My heart broke. "When was she here?" I asked as casually as I could, acting like this was not new information.

"A few weeks before you came out," she said. Reading my face, she went white. "Did he not tell you?"

I shook my head.

"Oh my God! Anna! I am so sorry! I should have kept my big mouth shut!"

I gave her a weak grin. "It's okay, Janet, no harm done." Which was a complete lie. The damage was catastrophic.

"I still feel bad. Mason is going to ream my ass for opening my mouth and butting in."

We got up from our spot and started to head back to the car. "We are grilling at our house tonight if you want to join us. Christian normally does."

"Sounds good to me," I replied. *I don't want to be alone with Christian anyway.*

An hour later, we were at their apartment, having a beer and sitting on their back patio when Mason and Christian pulled up. They came out to the back patio, and Janet launched herself at Mason. He laughed and smacked her butt before giving her a kiss. Christian walked up to me, and I stayed in my seat. He leaned down to kiss me, and I gave him my cheek. He pulled back, confused. "What is wrong, Anna?"

I took a pull from the beer and grinned at him. "Why would anything be wrong?"

The look he gave me let me know he knew I was full of it. He let it go anyway. *Good idea,* I thought.

After we ate and visited for a couple more hours, my attention stayed on anything but Christian, he was ready to go. We said our goodbyes and headed out. Once in the car, he sighed, "Something is wrong, just tell me, Anna."

I crossed my arms over my chest, hugging myself. "Why am I here, Christian?" I could feel the tears pooling in my eyes. *Damn it.*

"Because I wanted to see you, Anna. How many times do I have to say that to you?"

"Your intentions, Christian."

"What do you mean, my intentions? Intentions with what?"

*Fucking hell, I do not want to do this.* "I am here, you have seen me, now what?"

"I don't know," he said as he looked out the windshield.

I looked out my window so I didn't have to look at him. I didn't want to know the answer to what I was about to ask him. "Am I only here to keep you entertained for a week? Be your plaything, then send me home and never speak to me again?" By the time I finished asking, the tears were streaming down my face.

"Why the fuck would you ask me something like that, Anna?"

I shrugged. "Probably because Britt was here for the same amount of time as I am, only a few fucking weeks ago, Christian!" I was full-on crying now. "What happened, Christian? It didn't work out with her, so you took the next best thing? Or were you that bored that you shipped her home, and now it is my turn?"

"God, Anna, you make me sound like some sort of man whore." *If the shoe fits,* I thought to myself as he went on. "What were you expecting, Anna? What were your intentions coming out here?"

"Don't you dare turn this on me!"

"Answer me!" he yelled. It was the first time he had ever raised his voice at me. It scared me a little, but I would never let him know that.

"I don't know, Christian. I thought we would figure it out together."

# PIECE BY PIECE

"What is there to figure out?"

"I don't want you to say anything, Christian. My reason for being here is perfectly clear."

I slumped down in my seat, and we drove the rest of the way to his place in silence. When we got there, he headed straight for the shower, shutting the door behind him. A clear sign I was not to follow. *I don't want to anyway, asshole.*

I took the time to sit in the chair and read, not that I could pay any attention to the book. When he got out of the shower, he climbed into his bed and turned on the television, not even acknowledging that I was there.

I went to the shower so I could bawl my eyes out without him knowing. I ran the water hot and stood under it, shaking and crying until it went cold. I climbed out, dried off, and got dressed. When I came out, he was already asleep, his back to me. I sat in the chair by the bed and silently cried. Reality hit me like a freight train.

*Bud was right. I am just his plaything. Everything we shared together was a lie. At least on his end, it was. I loved him with everything I was. He was my hero, my protection, my safety. All I ever wanted was him, since I was fourteen years old. But to him, I am nothing but a toy, a fling when it fits into his plans. I am nothing. He never loved me. He never looked at his future and pictured me in it.*

I sat there watching the rise and fall of his chest, knowing his heart had never and would never beat for me, while mine was shattered from him. My safety blanket was going up in flames. The pain was so intense and then it turned to anger. *I bet if I told him the truth now, about what really happened, he wouldn't believe me or give a fuck. He probably wouldn't even bat an eye.* I felt the darkness coming, clouding my eyes. My chest tightened; I couldn't breathe. *I need to get away, now.*

I quietly packed my stuff so I wouldn't wake him. I got to the door and looked at him one last time, feeling all my dreams shatter and scatter around. "Goodbye, Christian. Even though you didn't, I have loved you since the day I met you. That will never change," I whispered into the dark room.

I shut the door quietly. My flight wasn't for two more days, but maybe I could switch it. I called a cab to pick me up down the road, and when I got in, I texted my mom. *Coming home early. Text you the information when I know.*

# PIECE BY PIECE

*Tonight is the night Bud broke me, with Christian's help. The night he pushed me so far into the darkness that I wasn't coming out of it.*

## CHAPTER 28

*Now*

A few days have passed since that phone call with Jack. I know he is close; I can feel it. He is waiting for the right time.

As I predicted, the calls from Jack to Josie's facility stopped. Rafe's parents took the girls on a 'vacation' since school is now out for the summer. Thank God. Jack will never find them.

Rafe and I sit on our deck drinking coffee, Bane at my feet. "How much longer do you think we will be putting up with this, Anna?" Rafe asks, his tone cold.

After telling him about the phone call with Jack at the facility, he has been on edge. "I can't answer that, Rafe."

## PIECE BY PIECE

"You think he will seriously try to kill you?" The look on his face breaks my heart.

Trying to make light of the situation, I smile. "He can try."

"That is not fucking funny, Anna."

I get up and go to where he is leaning against the rail. I circle my arms around his waist, squeezing him tight, feeling his warmth seep into me. "I love you, Rafe."

He kisses my forehead. "I love you too, Anna."

After all this time together, he still gives me butterflies. The look in his eyes is playful. "Want to show me how much you love me?" he asks.

I giggle. "You are worse than a teenage boy on prom night!"

He picks me up, throwing me over his shoulder, and smacks my ass. I squeal, then laugh. "Damn right, woman! Let's go!"

I wake up at three a.m. from another nightmare. This time Bud had my kids. I run my hands down my face, wiping the tears away. Rafe is out cold next to me. With his body bare from his waist up, one arm bent above his head, the other on his stomach, I can't help but stare. He is beautiful. I still don't understand how I got so lucky with him.

Our relationship has been a roller coaster ride from the start. *To hell and back.* With my fear and lack of trust in men, I did not make things easy for us. I was stubborn and always thought he was going to hurt me eventually. Every man who had come into my life had. When I got mad, my temper was horrible. I would scream, cry, and break things. Through every one of those episodes, Rafe was calm, which just made me more upset. To me, it seemed like he did not care at all, and didn't want to fight for us. He never said much, and I needed him to react, to communicate. Looking back now, him being that way was exactly what I needed.

Rafe never gives up. It's not in him to do that. He lets me rant and rave, but he never leaves. He never says it's too much or that he's done. He never walks away from me. His quiet strength keeps me from self-sabotaging behaviors. He is not perfect by any means, but for me, he is. God gives me what I need. He gives me Rafe, my silent, calm protector. He knows I can handle myself, and for the most part, he lets me, standing behind me just in case I need him.

## PIECE BY PIECE

We find what works for us, how to handle each other, and what we each need from the other. Being complete opposites, we balance each other out. For years I have been told we make the oddest couple. That might be true, I guess. What I know is true, is that Rafe is my only light in the darkness, my anxiety medicine, my calm during my storms, my true safety blanket. My love for him and our girls is unexplainable, unconditional. Knowing it is being threatened infuriates me. I will kill or be killed for them. It may just end up being one of those with Jack.

Needing fresh air, I put on my hot pink robe that the girls picked out for me last Christmas and head for our deck. The cold air hits me, and I take a deep breath of it. Sitting in one of our chairs, I overlook our property. I would be lying if I said I don't think of how my life would be different if I had made different choices, if I had chosen a different path. The reality is, without Rafe and our girls, I would be dead. I was on the road to self-destruction. I was suicidal. The depression I fought was overwhelming.

I wonder where I would be if I had told Christian the truth when we were kids. It has been twenty years now. Would we have stayed together? Gotten married? Had kids? Or would there have been something else to take him from me? *Does it even matter now? Every choice I made led me right here, where I am supposed to be, where God wants me to be.*

*Where would I be if I had made other choices? How would life be if what happened the night Bud died had never happened and he was still alive? Would he and my mom still be together?* Rafe would never allow him near our girls, but neither would I.

The sun is coming up, and I hear the sliding door open, then shut. *Rafe.* "Hey baby, are you okay?" he asks as he hands me a cup of coffee. The aroma and warmth from the mug feel so good.

"Bad dream."

"Want to talk about it?" He leans against the rail.

I shake my head. There is no point now.

"I thought I would go fishing today. Do you and Bane want to come with?"

"No, I think I will go for a run, then get some work done."

"Speaking of Bane, where is he?"

"Probably still sleeping."

"Weird for him to not be up your ass when you're awake." He grins at me.

"Jealous?"

He smirks, then shrugs. "Maybe."

He looks at me like I hurt his feelings, and we both burst out laughing. Finishing his coffee, he heads back to the door. "You going to be okay here alone when I go? I can stay home."

I shake my head. "No, I will be fine. Go ahead and go."

"Okay, well, my phone will be on. Just call me, and I will come right back."

I nod and finish my coffee.

I head inside to get dressed and go for my run as Rafe gets ready to go fishing. Bane is finally up and ready to go. I kiss Rafe goodbye and head to my trail.

Today, I am taking my time, walking most of it, and I am unsure why. *Maybe I am wanting to stay away from reality a bit longer. Take time to breathe in the fresh air.* Bane doesn't seem to mind it. We reach the top, and fog covers my view. The sun rises over the fog that covers the land, and I can't help but think of how beautiful it is. One of my favorite paintings of God's.

I stand there reflecting on all that has happened recently. *To say I am not scared would be a lie. Whoever goes through something like this and says they are not scared is full of it. Jack does not scare me as far as him hurting me. What scares me is if he hurts Rafe, my girls, or Bane. My world would be nothing without them.*

I am not scared to die, but I don't want to either. To never see my girls grow up, to never grow old with Rafe—that doesn't scare me; it pisses me off that I even have to think about it. The alternative is to just kill Jack myself. Even if it is self-defense, prison is not off the table. *At least I could see my girls grow up.*

"Whatever your plan is for me," I say to God, looking up at the sky, "I am ready. I trust in your plan, no matter the outcome. All I ask is that you keep Rafe, the girls, and Bane safe. I am ready to go to you if that is your plan, but I am also prepared to ask for your forgiveness again."

Taking a deep breath, I prepare to head home. I get down to Bane's level and put his big head in my hands. "Let's see what today brings us, big guy."

# PIECE BY PIECE

I take my time getting home, not wanting to be in the empty house alone. As I near the edge of the trail to my property, my house comes into view. The front door is wide open. *Weird.* Rafe's truck and boat are gone. I went out the back door when I left, so I didn't leave it open. I reach for my phone. *It's not here! Shit! I left it on the nightstand along with... fuck! Along with my gun.* I never forget either when I go out alone! I stay alongside my house when I hear steps at my front door. Bane growls, so I put him in the garage, and he begins to bark. "Anna! You might as well come out and face me!" *Fuck!* I step out into the yard and stay in view of our security cameras. *God, I hope Rafe decides to check them soon.* Jack walks into my doorway, one of Rafe's beers in his hand and a gun in the other. I stop where I am.

"We need to chat, little sister," he grins.

## CHAPTER 29

After the visit with Christian, I returned home to a smug Bud and a gloating Jack. I moved out of the house that same week, finding a tiny apartment forty-five minutes from their house. I worked two jobs and was in college full-time, going through life feeling numb. I still partied a lot. In doing so, I met Rachel and her husband, Nick. We hit it off, and Nick became like the older brother I always wanted but never had.

"Bar tonight, sis?" Nick called my cell phone.

"Sure! Main Street?"

"We'll be there!"

We hung up, and I called my mom, which had become an almost everyday thing, so I could keep watch over her and Josie. Josie answered the phone.

## PIECE BY PIECE

"Hey, my Jo-jo! How are you, sweetheart?"

"Um, I am okay. School sucks, but it is what it is."

Something was off with her; I could feel it and hear it in her tone.

"Josie, what's wrong?"

"Nothing, Anna," her tone getting defensive.

"Jo-jo, it's me; you can tell me."

She sighed. "Dad is just in a mood, and nothing I do is right."

"Has he hurt you?" I was immediately on alert.

"Nothing I can't or haven't handled before, Anna."

"Josie, tell someone. Call the cops; I will come get you!"

"I gotta go, Anna. Dad is home. Love you, bye."

The line went dead. *Son of a bitch! If I just show up, he will know she told me, and it will be worse for her.* I decided to stay where I was and wait for another call.

## PIECE BY PIECE

A few hours later, I was at the bar with Rachel and Nick, throwing down shots. "Hey, Anna!" I heard from the door. "Hey, Heidi!" Another friend of mine from college. We hugged, and I pulled up a seat for her.

"How are you?" I asked her as I passed out another round of Jack Daniels.

"Okay, I guess. David's ex is in the other room and is glaring at me, so this should be fun."

I followed her gaze to the other room, a bar with a door on each side separating the rooms. There were six girls in a group, staring us down. I smiled at them.

"Where is David?" I asked her.

"Working. I saw your car and decided to stop in, but I think I should go."

"Fuck that, Heidi! Stay with me; you'll be okay!" I announced in full drunken confidence.

After twenty minutes or so of shots with my friends, I decided to try and call Josie back. I slammed my drink and stepped outside to make the call.

"Hello?" My mom answered.

"Oh, hey Mom, it's Anna," I said, trying not to slur my words.

"Yeah, Anna, what do you need?" She was still pissed at me for getting a lawyer to try and get custody of Josie and sue Bud for the abuse. *I guess I can't really blame her.*

"Just wanted to talk to Jo-jo."

The line was quiet. "Mom?"

"Fuck you, bitch!" Bud screamed at me as he hung up the phone. *Remember to tell my lawyer that.*

"Ma'am?" I heard and turned to the road to see a police officer had pulled up beside me. "Are you okay?"

"Yeah, why?" I asked him, confused.

"Well, it's ten below and there is three feet of snow on the ground, and you are out here in just a hoodie."

I looked down at my clothes. *Well, hell.* "Just had to take this call, officer. I am heading back into the bar now. Thank you!"

He nodded and drove away. I noticed during my call I had walked a block from the bar. On the corner of the sidewalk, by the bar, I saw Heidi, surrounded by those six girls. All were yelling at her. *Fucking hell. Good thing I liquored up. Now I'm pissed and drunk. Fun times.* I ran to the group, sliding in the snow as I got in the middle with Heidi. "Holy shit!" I yelled, pointing to the cop who was driving away, "Y'all see that cop there?" They all looked, and I pushed Heidi out of the group, mouthing 'go' to her.

They all looked back at me. "Yeah? So what?" one said as they realized Heidi wasn't there anymore. I grinned.

"He just told me a farmer's cows got loose! You heifers better get back to your pasture, or we are all fucked!"

The first hit connected with my right eye. I blacked out. Not from the hit, but from the darkness when the anger in me came out to play. When I came back to, Nick had me flung over his shoulder, hauling me back to the bar. I started kicking and hitting his back, demanding to be put down so I could finish those bitches.

"Easy, sis!" He flopped me down in a seat at the bar.

"What?" I said to him as innocently as I could.

He laughed. "You dropped two of those 'heifers' as you call them, and were working on the third when I grabbed you out of the heap."

I frowned, crossing my arms over my chest. "I only got three? I thought there were six of them." I pouted.

"Anna, you were laughing the entire time!" Nick roared loudly. "I think you're done for the night, sis!"

On the other side of the bar, the six girls came back in and gathered, cussing and yelling at me. The three I got were bleeding. I reached over the bar and grabbed six shot glasses and the bottle of Jack Daniels. I poured all six and lined them up in a row.

"Anna! What the fuck!"

"Put it on my tab, Joe, it's fine!" I said as I picked up the first shot glass. I pointed it at the first girl, saluted her, and 'mooed'. By the time I got through to the sixth shot, I was being dragged out of the bar and shoved into Rachel's car.

"I love you, Anna, but fucking Christ, you are crazy!" Rachel yelled at me as the girls stumbled out of the bar. I laughed. We headed back to her house.

## PIECE BY PIECE

The next morning, my phone went off. *I hit ignore, I need sleep,* I thought. *I think I overdid it last night.* It rang again. I hit ignore again. The third time I was pissed and answered without looking to see who it was. "What!" I yelled.

"Anna?"

"Well, yeah, Mom, what do you need?" I snapped, copying her tone from last night.

"Is Josie with you?" Her voice was panicked and scared.

I sat straight up in bed. "No, she's not with me, Mom. What the fuck is going on?"

"She's fucking lying." I heard Bud yell in the background.

"Mom?"

"Please, Anna, if she is, we need to know," she said, practically in tears.

"She's not here, and I wouldn't lie about that. It wouldn't look good in court, Bud!" I yelled the last part into the phone.

I heard other voices and a radio. Police? "Mom, what the fuck?" Now I was starting to panic.

## PIECE BY PIECE

My mom was crying now. "She never got on the bus, Anna. She isn't at school and she isn't here. The police say there are tracks to the dirt road behind the house heading in your direction, but they lost the trail."

"I am on my way!" I jumped off the bed, looking for my keys and shoes.

"You are not welcome here!" Bud yelled.

"Fuck you, Bud!" I yelled back and hung up.

I made the forty-five-minute drive in under thirty minutes, fear and adrenaline rushing through me. When I pulled up, two squad cars and the officers, along with my mom and Bud, were standing in the driveway. I hopped out and met the officers.

"Anything new?"

"Not yet, Anna," the first officer answered. I had known him pretty much my whole life.

"Get off my property!" Bud practically spat at me. I flipped him off without even looking in his direction.

"Bud, stop! We need to focus on finding Josie!" my mom begged him. *I want to puke. How can she be like that?*

"Did you follow the tracks?" I asked the officer, ignoring Bud.

"It leads to the trail, but we can't follow it, and the tracks end there."

"Why can't you follow the tracks on the trail?" I asked, my temper flaring.

"The cars won't make that, and we do not have snowmobiles to go on it," he said, looking at all three of us.

"Are you fucking serious? Go to the bar, Frank! There are over five of them sitting there!" I yelled, losing my shit.

Frank held up his hands. "Anna, we have to wait."

"The fuck we do!" I took off to my truck.

Frank followed me. "Wait, Anna! You can't take this thing on that trail, it isn't safe!"

I threw the truck into drive. "Arrest me then, Frank! My little sister is missing out there in freezing cold temperatures and three feet of snow! I am not fucking waiting!" I took off.

I could see Josie's tracks and pulled onto the trail. "Fuck, Josie, where are you?" I said out loud. I followed the trail to an old bridge that was definitely not made for cars, let alone my truck. "Fuck it," I said to myself. I said a silent prayer, *if God is real, I might as well try.* I got halfway across the bridge and looked down to see the river below, with a minimum thirty-foot drop to water and boulders. I gripped the steering wheel.

Holding my breath, I slowly made it to the other side. Letting out a sigh of relief, I repeated 'Thank you' over and over as I continued down the trail. After seven miles down the trail, I started to really panic. *I hope she was smart enough to stick with the trail,* I thought, as her tracks were no longer visible with the new snow falling down.

I looked ahead and saw a dark figure. *Josie!* I hit the gas and pulled up alongside her as she stared at me in shock. "Anna? What are you doing here?"

"Josie, get in the truck!" I demanded. Seeing she was fine, the panic faded and anger set in.

"I am not going back to that house!" she yelled at me, tears rolling down her face. Her stance was defensive.

## PIECE BY PIECE

"Get in the damn truck where it's at least warm, and we'll talk, okay?" I said as calmly as I could.

She climbed in, throwing her big backpack in the back seat. When she did, she winced. "What's wrong?" I asked her. The look she gave me let me know she was scared to tell me because I was not going to like it. "Josie, please. You have everyone scared. The cops are at the house. Mom called me, that's how scared they are for you."

She sighed and took off her gloves. Her hands shaking, she held them out to me. All along her fingers from knuckle to fingertip were cut, bruised, or both. The swelling had already started. I was in shock and needed to register what I was looking at. Then she lifted her shirt. Bruising on her ribs and a perfect boot imprint on her back, already bruising. The look on my face was enough, she panicked. "Anna please, don't do anything to him!" She was practically begging me.

"Why, Josie? What was the excuse for this?" I said, pointing to her hands and then her back. Chewing on her lower lip, the tears were coming down hard. "Josie, tell me. Now." It was the last time I was going to ask her, but even the calmness and edge in my voice scared me.

## PIECE BY PIECE

"Dad and mom were arguing about you filing for custody of me and the accusations against him. They called me into the living room and asked why I would make up those lies. I told them I didn't know anything about it, and Dad didn't believe me. He grabbed me by my hair and threw me to the ground. When I tried to get up, he would kick me back down. Mom tried to stop him, and he hit her too. I tried to get away, Anna, I swear I did. But he kicked me again, and I couldn't get up." She was telling me this through sobs and gasping for air, "He took me to the barn, and he made me place my hands on his workbench. He took the straight edge of a ruler and for every accusation you accused him of, he would hit my hands. He made me repeat the accusations after each hit and say it was a lie. If I took too long or if I tried to pull my hands away, he hit me." I was crying by the time she finished telling the story. Her hands looked broken.

"Why didn't you go to school and tell them? Or call me?" I said through my tears.

Josie shook her head. "No one would believe me, they never do. You know that, and I didn't know your number. Dad won't let me have it."

My grip on the steering wheel was so tight, I felt like it might snap. The anger, hatred, and disgust I had for this man were unexplainable. I put the truck in drive and started for the road. "Where are we going?" Josie asked, her eyes huge with fear.

I looked at her, hating my own answer. She started bawling and screaming again. "Anna! No! Please! I can't go back! He will kill me!" The fear in her voice fueled my anger. "The police are there, Josie. We can tell them what happened, and I will call my lawyer." She was shaking in the passenger seat. "Jojo, he will never hurt you again, you hear me? He will have to kill me first."

My phone dinged. 'Have you found her?' my mom texted me. I bit back my rage. 'Yes, we are heading back now.' *Little did I know how crucial my reply to her would be.*

We pulled up to the house and my mom and Bud came out. I noticed the police cars were gone. *Convenient for Bud.* I looked at Josie. "Stay in the truck for a bit." I climbed out, shutting my door.

"Where are the police, Mom?"

"You said you had found her and because you never asked for help or an ambulance, we all assumed she was fine, so

# PIECE BY PIECE

they left and said to call them if we needed. They are reporting it as a runaway."

"Call them back, now, Mom," my temper reached its tipping point.

"Why? She's safe, right?"

I noticed Bud was standing back behind my mom a few feet. I glared at him. "Not even fucking close. Have you seen her hands? Her ribs or her back? Better yet, Mom, tell me about the bruise you're hiding!"

She stepped back away from me. "Honestly, Anna, this needs to stop!"

"Now wait, Anna..." Bud finally stepped in.

"Fuck you, Bud! You're going to fucking jail!" I yelled. Then I heard the truck door open and slam shut.

"Anna, it's okay. It's my fault," Josie said from behind me.

"Girl! You gave your mom a fucking heart attack, what the fuck! I am going to teach you what happens when you do stupid shit!" Bud went off on Josie.

## PIECE BY PIECE

I turned to Josie and grabbed her shoulders to look her in the eyes. "Josie—" I started.

"Get in the fucking house, Josie, now!" Bud yelled, getting closer to us.

"—you want to play hide and seek?" I asked her. Her eyes went huge as she understood what I meant. I gave her a light shove toward the house. "Go, Jo-jo." She took off into the house.

My mom was standing there, doing nothing but crying. I rolled my eyes at her, then turned to Bud. "How about I teach you a lesson, Bud, when you do stupid shit!"

He laughed. "Yeah right, little girl! What the fuck are you gonna do?"

I raised one eyebrow at him, then looked at my mom who was standing there like a deer in headlights. I snickered at him and then went back to my truck to grab my phone. I dialed 9-1-1 as I turned back to my mom and Satan.

"Who are you calling? Backup?" Bud said, laughing.

"Hi, yes, I need to report child abuse. The address is—" Bud hit the phone out of my hand. "You little cunt!"

"Bud, stop!" my mom begged him.

I took a fist to the face and hit the ground. He grabbed me by my hair, jerking me back up to my feet. The pain was excruciating. Slamming me into my tailgate, he put his hands around my neck and started squeezing.

"Bud, stop! You're going to kill her!" my mom screamed, pulling at his arms, trying to get him off me. I didn't struggle; I smiled at him, unable to breathe. He let me go with one hand and backhanded my mom, knocking her to the ground.

I blacked out then. The anger, rage, and darkness were too much for me. I heard nothing, saw nothing, felt nothing. When I came to, I was standing over Bud's body, blood gushing from his head. My mom was holding him, screaming. There was blood all over my hands, my right holding the tire iron that was also covered in his blood. The sirens were getting closer. I dropped the tire iron and held my hands above my head, perfectly calm.

Three weeks later, I was in court, waiting to hear the verdict of guilty or not guilty for the murder of Bud. My lawyer did an amazing job of proving self-defense, and with Josie's statement, plus physical evidence of the abuse she had endured,

I had hope. Even if found guilty, I would smile and say it was worth it because now Josie and my mom were safe. I no longer had to worry.

Jack and Rhea sat behind the prosecuting attorney. I had to listen to Jack's testimony about how I should get the death penalty because I had robbed him of his 'Daddy'. I tried so hard not to roll my eyes, focusing on the judge instead of listening to his whining. My mom gave a statement but refused to read it or go on the stand. It surprised me that they didn't make her, but I was okay with it. She was at least here, to my surprise, and sitting behind me.

I refused a plea deal and decided I would rather take my chances at trial. Yes, I did kill him, but I would not plead guilty to murder when I was protecting my mom and sister. As I reflected on my life, while waiting to hear my fate, I wondered what would have happened if I had made different choices. Would my life still have led me to this moment? Probably, with the way Bud was.

"Ms. Paxton," the judge said, pulling me from my thoughts. I stood, the cuffs heavy on my small wrists.

## PIECE BY PIECE

"The jury finds the defendant, not guilty," he read, and the breath I didn't realize I had been holding escaped from me in a rush. My mom burst into tears, and Jack jumped out of his seat. "This is fucking bullshit! She is a goddamn murderer!" he yelled, his face red with anger. The whole courtroom looked at him as he glared at me. *I smile.*

"You need to calm down, son, or you will be found in contempt!" the judge ordered.

The judge continued, "This was a clear case of self-defense. Ms. Paxton, I am so sorry for the pain and fear you and your family have had to endure for so many years. The charges for murder will be destroyed and not on your record. I ask that you do something with your life, Ms. Paxton. Do not waste it. You are free to go."

Tears started to fall as the deputy removed my cuffs. "Yes, sir." I hugged my lawyer, then Josie.

Jack stormed out of the courtroom, the door slamming against the wall. As I walked to the entrance to leave, I came upon my mom and Rhea. My mom hugged me. "Anna, I am so sorry, I tried—"

"Mom, he hurt you too. You were scared of him just like we were. I do not blame you."

She hugged me tightly, then looked at me, cupping my face in her hands. "Where you got your strength, I have no clue. God must have given you that. You sure didn't get it from me." I said nothing.

I turned to face Rhea, not sure what to do or say. She hugged me. "I don't know what to say, Anna. He was my dad, and I loved him. The way he treated us was bad. You always stood up to him, from the very beginning you protected us."

I gave her a small smile. "It's okay, Rhea. I get it. I understand if you want nothing to do with me after all this. I love my dad too, even if he isn't a 'real dad', so I see where you are coming from."

"Ms. Paxton?" My lawyer said, coming up behind me. I turned to see him and two officers, and I sighed. "I literally have not left this building! What did I do now?"

All three of them smiled. My lawyer stepped forward. "No, Anna. I have asked these two to take you to your car. I worry about Jack."

## PIECE BY PIECE

I shrugged. *Jack doesn't scare me; he never has.* "Ready?" I heard my mom say.

I turned back to her and Josie. "Very ready."

We got to the car when I heard two loud pops, then four more. *Those are gunshots!* "Anna! Oh my God, baby! Don't move! Hang on!" My mom screamed at me, holding me.

"Why?" I asked her. *Why are we on the ground now?* Then I felt the pain and looked down to see my shirt covered in blood. *Well, fuck, I've been shot.*

I heard Josie screaming for help as I looked around to see who did it. Jack was on the ground; the two cops had him cuffed. He was screaming like he was hurt. *They must have shot him too.*

He looked at me. "I hope you die and go to hell, bitch!"

I grinned. "I'll tell your dad you said hello." My head fell back; damn, the pain was bad. I could feel it in my shoulder, chest, stomach, everywhere.

"Stay awake, baby! The ambulance is almost here!" My mom cried, looking at me as she cradled my face. Josie was at my legs, in tears.

I looked up at them and smiled a weak smile. "The bastard shot me," I laughed. "Who knew he had balls?" Then I blacked out.

I came to in a hospital, my mom at my bedside. When she saw I was awake, she jumped up. "Anna! Oh, thank God!"

"Did I die?"

She laughed through her tears. "No, baby. Jack shot you twice, one in your shoulder and the other in your side. You lost a lot of blood, but no major organs were hurt. That was three days ago, baby."

"Oh, okay. He's a shitty shot then, huh?" I said, laughing.

"Yes, thank God for that. He's in jail. He was shot in the leg, but he can recover in prison," she said to me with a smile.

"How is Josie?" I asked.

"I'm just fine, Anna. Worry about yourself for once," she said, coming from the door.

"Never," I said.

A year later, we were in court for Jack's attempt to kill me. I made sure to sit where he could see me. He stared me down, looking like a kid who got tattled on. I didn't acknowledge him. They took his plea deal, and he was sentenced to thirty years with the possibility of parole for good behavior. His attorney stated it was not premeditated. *Bullshit,* I thought, chuckling to myself.

As they took him away, he grinned at me. "This is not over," he whispered as he walked by.

# CHAPTER 30

*Now*

Making sure I stay in full view of the cameras and praying Rafe looks at them soon, I stare at Jack.

"First off, I am NOT your sister and second, I have nothing to 'chat' with you about," I tell him, keeping my calm and steady. *It's hard to do when a gun is pointed at me.*

He rolls his eyes, "Well, I do want to chat. We have a lot to discuss."

I fold my arms over my chest, huffing out my breath and rolling my eyes, "I am not taking on any new clients Jack, besides, what you need is beyond my professional abilities."

I see his jaw clench. *Man, he looks like his piece of shit dad.* "Still a smartass I see."

I shrug, "Old habits and all that, Jack."

I can hear Bane barking and slamming himself into the door to the garage. Jack steps away from my front door in my direction. He looks at the garage quickly then back at me.

"Good thing you put up the mutt, although killing him in front of you would be fun."

I sigh, acting like what he is saying and doing has no effect on me, "Jack, seriously, I am bored, talk or leave."

"Shut the fuck up! I am the one with the gun! I give the orders, not you!" He yells, his eyes bugging out of his head. *He almost looks stoned.*

I snicker, "That's a first, you giving the orders. Tell me, Jack, is it a lot better than being the one that takes them?"

He takes a few more steps closer, closing the gap, "I like to give the orders, especially to you!"

I cock my head to the side, looking like I am confused, "You're the big tough guy now that 'daddy' isn't here to do it?"

He growls, "You cunt!" *He really does look like Bud, almost his twin.*

He takes another couple of steps towards me. *Yeah, dumbass, keep getting closer,* I think to myself.

"I think after I kill you and your mutt, I will hang you from the tree for your husband and girls to find." He says grinning at me. His gun is pointed at my stomach and he is shaking. *That can be good or bad, I am not sure yet which it is.*

"Is that what you wanted to 'chat' about, Jack?" I ask, not taking my eyes off his.

He shakes his head and lets out a low whistle, "Where do we start, Anna? Do we start with how you murdered my dad or how I sat in prison, for years, dreaming of this day? Or even better, let's 'chat' about how I am surprised by you!"

I wrinkle my nose at that one, confused. He grins at my face which shows confusion.

"See, me and my dad had a bet. I bet you would end up killing yourself, especially after what he did about you and Christian. Which was brilliant, by the way. Dad bet that you would end up marrying that prick and become his toy for life, living in misery. That always pissed him off, though, because he hated Christian so bad. Which made his plan to break y'all up even better."

I say nothing and do not react, *like I was trained to do, thanks to Bud.*

"We were both wrong, Anna! He would roll over in his grave knowing you ended up some hotshot therapist, married with two kids from the same man you're still married to. Living in this—" He says as he waves his hand around at my house. "Impressive, but I do wonder one thing?"

"You wonder how your dad can roll over while he rots in hell? Bet that hurts him," I say, grinning.

His beady eyes go black, his voice cold, "You know you will visit him soon. But no, I wonder how your family would feel about you, knowing you're still in love with Christian. Living a lie."

I burst out laughing. "I am not—"

"Don't lie, Anna. You are. You still follow his social media, and you fantasize about what life with him would be like if Dad hadn't forced you to dump him."

# PIECE BY PIECE

"Jack, I'm starting to think it was you two who were in love with him. I mean, it has been twenty years, and you still bring him up, still trying to throw him in my face. Bud did me a favor."

His grin is back. "Okay, whatever you say, sis, but it's nice to know he won't be here to save you this time. In fact, I doubt he even blinks when he hears you're dead."

I shrug. "Well, Jack, for the first time ever, we agree on something. But I save myself like I always have."

"Not this time, this time you will get what you deserve."

"To kill you? Make sure you tell your dad I said hi," I say, surprised by how calm I am being with this.

He backhands me, whipping my head back. *Instantly, I am fourteen again, facing Bud.*

"I'm going to kill you!" Jack yells, grabbing my throat and squeezing. "But first I'm going to beat you worse than my dad ever did!" He points the gun against my head.

The metallic taste in my mouth is strong. I grin. "You have never been able to do that, Jack, so don't kid yourself."

He hits me again, this time with the gun, across my face. I hit the ground. Through the blood and tears, I see Jack put the gun in his waistband at the small of his back. *Good job, dumbass,* I think to myself.

"I don't need the gun; I think I would prefer killing you with my bare hands," he says as he grabs me by my hair.

I take that opening and uppercut him, watching his head snap back. His grip on my hair doesn't loosen at all.

"Fucking bitch!" he growls and punches me in my gut.

I double over and feel like I am going to puke. I cough and then pretend to cry, staying hunched over, grabbing my stomach. He still has my hair and is panting like a dog.

"Aww, Anna, don't cry," he laughs as he punches me in the face again, this time releasing my hair as I fall to my hands and knees.

Blood is coming from my nose and mouth, covering the ground beneath me. He gives me a kick to the ribs, rolling me to my back. I try to catch my breath as he stands over me.

"Come on, Anna! I know you can fight better than this! This is too easy!" he yells at me.

## PIECE BY PIECE

I pray to myself as I look up to the sky, *Tell me what to do, God. Help me.*

I roll back onto my knees and stagger to my feet. Jack cheers me on, "There ya go! Good job, Anna!" He laughs and taunts me.

I stand to my full height, which isn't much, and spit blood out of my mouth. "Alright, Jack, let's fight." He grins at me.

"This is going to be amazing! Killing you slowly, I can enjoy it!" He taunts me again.

I charge him, dropping low. I throw my shoulder into his hips and tackle him to the ground.

"Damn! You should have played football, sis!" He laughs as he lies on the ground.

My body is half his size. I sit myself up on him and punch him as hard as I can, connecting to his face. Blood instantly pours from his nose.

We roll around, swapping punches like two kids on a playground. The gun falls from his waistband. I dive for it, and he grabs my foot, pulling me away from it. By now, we are close to the garage.

## PIECE BY PIECE

"Oh no, no, Anna! That is cheating!"

I roll to my back and kick him in the stomach. He curses and drags me farther from the gun. He grabs me by my hair again, punching me in the face again. The world spins on me.

As I struggle to keep from passing out, Jack smiles at me, "Time is up, Anna. Dad is waiting for you."

He leaves me to go get the gun. "Your time is up, Jack!" I yell at him, stopping him.

He turns back to me. "Anna, are you serious? You can barely stand up! You want to keep fighting?"

I smile, *at least I think I am.* "Not me," I tell him. He looks at me, confused, *thinking I have lost my mind.*

I whistle as loud as I can. "Bane! Come!"

"He is in the—"

The glass window to the garage shatters as Bane comes through it, his feet hitting the ground at a dead run, his teeth bared.

"Fuck!" Jack yells, running for the gun.

# PIECE BY PIECE

Bane reaches him as he reaches the gun. Bane latches onto his arm, thrashing around with it, the gun falling. Jack punches him with his other hand, but Bane isn't phased. Jack falls to the ground with Bane over him.

I call Bane to me, and he releases Jack, coming to me.

Jack is holding his arm, screaming, "He broke my fucking arm!"

Sirens sound. *Rafe. 'Thank God,'* I think to myself. "It's over, Jack," I say as I walk towards him, looking for the gun. He pulls it from behind him, pointing it at Bane. "Mutt first!"

"No!" I yell as the darkness takes me over again. I hear a shot and feel the pain. He shot me in the same fucking shoulder! He shoots again and misses. "Fuck you, Anna!" He yells as I charge him.

"Bane!" I yell, and he is at my side. Jack pulls the trigger, nothing. He tries again, nothing. It's jammed. I clear the gap between us, kicking the gun out of his hand. He swings at me with his good arm, but I dodge it. I punch him, hard. He grabs my shoulder and squeezes the gunshot wound.

I scream from the pain. I fall to the ground. "Bane! Kill him!"

I lay there as the sirens get louder. They almost drown out Jack's screams as Bane has his good arm now, shaking him like a toy.

"Bane, hold!" I order. Bane stops and holds his bite, not easing up.

"Get him off me!" Jack screams.

"If I do, will you stop?"

"Yes!"

"You will leave me, my family, Josie, everyone alone?"

Jack growls in pain, "Fuck you! I will hunt you till one of us is dead!"

"Anna!" Rafe screams from behind me at a dead run for me. I turn to look at him and hear Jack laugh. I turn back, and he has the gun pointed at Bane's head. It clicks again, still jammed. Jack looks at it, confused.

"Bane," I say calmly as Jack looks at me with pure hate on his face. "Kill him." Bane releases Jack's arm and lunges for his throat. He shakes him until the screaming and gurgling stop. It gets quiet. "Bane, release. Come." I sink to my knees as Bane reaches me, Rafe just a few seconds behind him.

"Oh shit, Anna! Hold on! Help is coming!" I fall to the side, into Rafe. The pain is unbearable now that the adrenaline is subsiding.

"Rafe?"

"Yeah, baby?"

"I love you."

He hugs me tight. "I love you too, but hold on!"

I start to sag in his arms. *I am so tired.*

"Stay awake, Anna! They are here, hold on!"

"Bane?" I ask. I have lost so much blood. "He is here, baby, we both are," Rafe says, crying.

## CHAPTER 31

*Two months later...*

Since that day, I had to undergo two surgeries. I ended up with a concussion and a brain bleed, and the bullet hit my shoulder just right. I lost a lot of blood between the beating to my head and the bullet wound. The doctor was surprised at the recovery I made. "I have never seen anyone fight the way you did, let alone recover this fast with the injuries you had."

"Apparently you don't know my wife," Rafe says with a grin.

I roll my eyes. "That was all God himself, not me." I lay in the hospital with Bane in my bed.

"I still can't believe you convinced them to let you have him in here," Rafe says, shaking his head and chuckling.

# PIECE BY PIECE

"I told them to fight me," I say with a smile.

"Of course you did, babe," Rafe says with a sigh.

The nurse walks in with her hands on her hips. "Between the phone calls and that mutt, I will be glad when you are released, missy!"

I cover Bane's ears and fake a shocked look. "Don't listen to her, Bane, you're not a mutt! She's just jealous!" I hug Bane, him rolling onto his back into my lap. "You are the most beautiful man I know, Bane!"

"Thanks, Babe," Rafe says, laughing. The nurse looks at us, annoyed. I smile at her and shrug.

"Seriously, Anna, the media is blowing up our phones! Have you even given the police your statement?" she says, checking my monitors and giving Bane a quick pat on his head. "You're awfully popular, young lady!"

I let my head fall back onto my pillow, staring at the ceiling. "What do you mean?"

When I don't get an answer, I look at Rafe then the nurse, and back to him. "Well, what does she mean, Rafe? Popular how?"

## PIECE BY PIECE

"You don't know yet?" she asks, looking at Rafe, her face confused but also panicked. "You haven't told her?"

"Know what!" I yell, and Bane whimpers. I pet him and shush him to let him know I am fine.

Rafe stands and runs his hands through his hair. "So, you stayed within our cameras throughout the whole fight with Jack, right?" I nod. "It was all caught on it and recorded."

"Yeah, so? Now the police have it, so what does that matter? Was it somehow released when it shouldn't have been?" I ask, as my anxiety starts to take over, my heart rate monitor speeding up.

Rafe shakes his head. "The camera footage was not released, Anna."

"Okay, then what?"

"Jack had his own way of livestreaming it all. I think to broadcast what you did to Bud and everyone can see him be the one to avenge his dad." Rafe's eyes look at me, sad and angry.

My heart monitor speeds up, the nurse comes over. "Sweetheart, you need to calm down, but you should also know that it went viral."

## PIECE BY PIECE

I have an instant panic attack, my breathing becomes harder, pain in my chest. The nurse administers something to help calm me down, though I don't know what it is.

Bane is now in my face, licking and nudging me softly. I grab him and hold on for dear life with my good arm. "Oh my God, the girls! What is this going to do to them?"

"They will be fine, Anna. They are strong like you. They know what you did was to protect all of us," Rafe says, rubbing my arm. I nod; he is right.

"You are a very blessed woman. You have an amazing husband who adores you, along with your kids," the nurse says, waving at Bane, "and this mutt, plus the support of millions of people. And God himself."

I give her a weak smile; she is right. I try to calm down as I take in what I have learned in a matter of minutes.

"Wait. Millions of people?" I ask, confused.

She grins. "Well, yeah, that livestream made you and Bane heroes, hun. Especially to women and kids who have or are going through what you did."

I look at Rafe, and he shrugs as the nurse continues, "Do you realize how many people you have helped? How many can relate to your story? Your story isn't even fully out yet, and you have already saved lives."

The tears come down as I shake my head. "I am not a hero, not even close. Bane maybe, but not me. I just did what I had to do to see my family again."

Rafe kisses my forehead. "You are my hero. I am so proud of you and Bane."

"You need rest, little one," the nurse says as I feel the medication she gave me kick in. My head falls back to the pillow, and I am out.

A few hours later, I wake up, and Rafe is still there, looking out the window of my hospital room. He looks scared or sad; I can't tell.

"What are you worrying about, Rafe?" I ask him.

He turns back to me and comes to the bed, taking my hand. "I thought I had lost you, Anna."

"Rafe—" he puts his hand up to stop me.

"I did, and that was the scariest moment of my life. I honestly thought you were going to die." His voice catches, and tears pool in his eyes. "Anna, I love you so damn much. My life would be nothing without you."

"I love you too, Rafe."

"You know, I have probably watched that damn video a thousand times," Rafe admits, looking at me. "I know you love me, but was Jack right?"

"About what?"

"Are you still in love with this Christian guy, or wish it was him you are with?"

I chew on my bottom lip, tears falling. "Rafe, I don't even know who he is anymore. He was the first person I ever truly loved, yes. That has stuck with me my whole life and never really gone away." He looks away, but I continue, "But I loved and remember the boy he was. I love the man you are. I do believe Bud cheated us, but I also think Christian meant way more to me than I ever did to him. I know what I was to him and what he was for me, and they are not the same. All of that is the past. You, our girls, and Bane are my now, my future, my forever. My broken puzzle is complete since I met you."

Rafe nods, tears slipping from his eyes. "I can't lose you, Anna, in any way, to anyone."

I grin. "Except Bane, right?"

Rafe lets out a grunt and rolls his eyes. "Damn dog, never thought that would be my competition."

We both laugh as Bane barks in response.

## CHAPTER 32

Two weeks later, I am released from the hospital. During those two weeks, I was questioned probably a dozen times by police about how, what, and why everything led up to that day with Jack. I was told I was going on house arrest during recovery and until my court hearing.

As we are getting ready to leave, two officers come into my room. "We are here to escort you home," the first officer says, his tag reading 'Martinez' and he looks barely old enough to be out of high school.

"I'm not a flight risk, kid," I say dryly.

"I don't doubt that, ma'am, but we need to make sure you make it through the parking lot and home safely," he says before eyeing Bane. "Is that dog going to hurt me or anyone?"

# PIECE BY PIECE

I leash Bane and sigh, "He has been here the whole time and hasn't hurt anyone. Plus, I won't tell him to, so he won't. And what do you mean, make it through the parking lot and home safely?"

The second officer steps forward, his tag reading 'Banks'. "There are hundreds waiting outside to see you and your dog, ma'am." I roll my eyes, Rafe laughs, "I'll bring the Jeep around back; maybe we can sneak out." He leaves to get the Jeep as the nurse comes in. "You and the mutt ready, kid?" She giggles as she hands Bane a dog treat. "I'll miss this big boy for sure," she says as she hands him another treat. She hugs me after Bane's attention from her is done. "Go be their angel, darling."

"No, but the only reason I'm even alive is from God himself," I tell her, taking a deep breath.

"Amen."

We get out to the Jeep, which we got back from repairs while I was in the hospital, with cop cars behind us and one in front of us. "Seriously?" I ask Rafe, looking behind us and in front of us at the cop cars.

Rafe nods, "Just wait, babe."

# PIECE BY PIECE

We pull around the back of the hospital and start up the street. As we do, I can see the front of the building. "Holy shit!" I gasp as I see over a hundred people in the parking lot, half of them looking like news crews.

Some of the crowd is holding signs that read 'His fist is big, but my Bane is bigger!' and 'End Domestic Violence, be like Anna!'

I shake my head and read them to Rafe. "The Bane one is clever, I guess," Rafe says, smiling.

"Well, I'll sing that song that way from now on then," I say sarcastically.

The crowd notices us and turns toward our direction, beginning to run. The cops aren't helping with their damn lights on and driving like we are in a parade. I tell Rafe to get us out of here and quick, *my anxiety going ninety to nothing.*

"Sorry, Officer," he says as he hits the gas and veers around the one in front. I look behind to see both squad cars speeding up to keep pace with Rafe. When we clear town, the officer who was in front takes his place there again.

"This is insane, Rafe," I say as I rest my head on the seat and close my eyes.

"Yeah, um, home is no better, love."

I lift my head and stare at him. "Fucking great."

We pull up to the house and are greeted with news crews at our gated entrance. There was a group on the road, but I didn't think they could get to our house, thank God.

Police block our drive, even though it is gated. I get out of the Jeep and take a look around, specifically where Jack had bled out. Nothing is there, not even police tape.

Rafe takes my hand. "You ok?"

I nod, not moving. "I feel nothing, Rafe. No sadness, no regret, nothing. Is that wrong? Shouldn't I feel something?" He says nothing.

"Ma'am?" Officer Banks says from behind me.

"Yeah, officer."

"There will be an officer stationed here around the clock until the hearing. We can't risk anyone getting out."

## PIECE BY PIECE

"Or me taking off?" I ask as I turn to him.

"Unless it is a medical emergency, no, ma'am, you can't leave or take off," he says, not smiling.

"Way to catch the sarcasm, Banks. Good job."

"No reason to laugh, ma'am. You are also not allowed to speak, write, email, or post to social media at all until after the hearing. Your lawyer will contact you and tell you the same thing."

I salute him. He gives me an irritated stare, then leaves.

"You're not helping, Anna," Rafe says.

"Don't give a fuck, Rafe."

"I know."

The door to my house opens, and we get closer to it. "Mommy!" my girls scream in unison as they barrel toward me. I laugh and hold my left arm open, the right still in a sling, and the girls almost tackle me as Rafe tells them to calm down. It hurts like hell, but I don't care; I am back with my girls.

Dee backs up, looking at me sternly. "You could have died, Mom."

"Yeah, I know, Dee, but I didn't. God and Bane protected me. I'm sorry you had to deal with this," I say with all sincerity. Her face softens. I am forgiven.

Jessie is bouncing all over the place. "Mom! You kicked his butt! Bane just finished him off."

I whip my head to Rafe, staring at him coldly. He holds both his hands up in surrender. "I don't know how they know; I didn't show them anything, I swear."

"It's all over the internet, Mom," Dee pipes up.

"Okay, no more internet for you two without supervision."

Jessie already has her attention on Bane. "My hero!" she yells as he licks her face.

# CHAPTER 33

The next week and a half are slow, thank goodness. Rafe goes back to work, so I focus on homeschooling the girls. Better for them to stay home with me than to deal with school issues anyway. Rafe's parents stay with us to help since I am still healing while also working from home on top of teaching the girls.

Working from home is difficult, not because we have to video chat, but because every client wants to focus on Jack and me, not themselves. I also spend a lot of time with my lawyer to go over the hearing and the process. The main issues in the case are to prove that it was self-defense and justified and that Bane is not a threat to society since he killed Jack.

"But he saved my fucking life!" I say, basically hysterical.

"Everyone knows that, Anna. Anyone who knows you or Bane knows his training and how good he is. They just have to look at everything, and there are a few nomads on the internet saying Bane should be put down. Which means if he is found a risk, he will be euthanized."

"Over my dead body! They have to kill me first!"

"Anna, calm down, let's cross that bridge when and if we get to it."

Sensing my anxiety, Bane comes over and lays his head in my lap. I press my forehead to his. "Nothing will happen to you, Bane, unless it happens to me first." He licks my cheek.

That night my dad calls to catch up since I never have time anymore to just chat. "Hey, baby girl! How are you doing, hun?"

I smile; his loud deep voice is so amazing to me. Most think he is too loud, and he is most of the time, but I love it. "I am okay, Dad, healing quickly. How are you?"

"Worried, Anna. You know your brother and I will be there to kick anyone's ass who needs it—"

I laugh, a soft half-hearted laugh. That is just like them, wanting to kick someone's ass for me.

"—your mom told me about this hearing and the whole Bane issue."

I look at Bane, who is sleeping on the couch across the room. "They can't kill him, Dad. I would never make it."

"They won't, honey."

"How can you be so sure, Dad?"

"When have I ever made you a promise I didn't keep?" he says, his voice cracking a little.

"Never, Daddy."

The line goes quiet. "Dad? What's wrong?" I ask, nervous.

I hear his intake of breath, and then he answers, "I have never been so scared, Anna. I thought you were going to die when I first watched the video—"

"Dad, I didn't die—"

"Let me finish, girl—"

# PIECE BY PIECE

"Yes, Daddy—"

"I felt hopeless. Your brother and I want to protect you like you should have been protected your whole life, but we weren't there. Even knowing he was there, stalking you and tormenting you, and then this. I should have been there, Anna. If it wasn't for Bane—" He stops to take a deep breath, and I can hear him wipe his nose. "If it wasn't for that damn dog, I would have lost you. That would have destroyed me and your brother too. I have been playing that song you love so much, the one you said reminds you of me, on repeat since the incident with Jack. What was it called again? Some country song?"

I start crying, "Piece by Piece, Dad, by Kelly Clarkson."

"That's it! It reminds me how lucky I am to have you as my kid. You will get through this, baby girl. I will help you. You are strong, stubborn, and obviously a fighter. I don't tell you enough, but I am proud of you, Anna."

I am bawling at this point. "Thanks, Daddy," I say through ragged breaths.

"Tell her I will fucking be at court, and God help anyone who tries anything fucking stupid!" I hear my brother yell through the phone.

# PIECE BY PIECE

Dad laughs, "I think she heard you, son. Anna? Want to say hello to your asshole of a brother?"

I laugh. "Yeah, Dad."

"She better have said, 'Hell yeah, I want to talk to my favorite person ever!'" My brother says as he takes the phone.

"Her favorite person is Bane, smartass. You can't compete with that!" My dad yells back.

I am laughing so hard now; these two never give me a dull moment.

After I talk with my brother, we say our goodbyes and 'see you soons.'

# CHAPTER 34

It's the day of my hearing, and the turnout for it is insane. Hundreds of people are outside chanting and holding signs: 'Bane is a hero!' and 'Anna is the light in our dark!' I am overwhelmed, and the support from strangers is something I will never get used to.

In the courtroom, I am overrun with newscasters. My lawyer and the police help me through to our table. I turn around to see who is here that I know. There isn't one empty seat in this courtroom. Rafe and his parents are behind me. My mom, dad, and brother are next to them. I give everyone a small smile before I turn back around.

The bailiff announces us to rise for the judge, and we stand. I feel nothing, hear nothing. It feels like I am dreaming.

The judge comes in and we take our seats. *Here we go,* I think to myself as we get started.

"So, am I going to have to tell my entire story to everyone here, aren't I?" I whisper to my lawyer, ignoring the prosecuting attorney's opening statement.

"Basically, yes. You can do it, Anna," he whispers back.

"Call your first witness," the judge announces to my attorney. *Fuck, here we go.*

"I would like to call Doctor Anna Garrison to the stand, please," my attorney announces.

I stand and walk to the stand, taking in all the people. I want to puke; my nerves are shot and my heart won't slow down. I take a deep breath and raise my right hand. *God, I need you with me, please,* I think to myself, knowing He hears me. I focus all my attention on my lawyer.

"Anna, do you understand why you are here and the charges against you?"

"Yes, I know."

## PIECE BY PIECE

"Can you start by telling us about your educational background along with your profession?"

I list it all off as if reading my resume to everyone. I can tell by a few faces that they are impressed as if I give a shit.

"Why did you choose psychology?"

"So I can help others work through their trauma. To let them know they are heard, understood, and believed. And also so I could take my dog to work with me," I answer, smiling.

"Your dog Bane?"

"Not at first; my first was Bowser, a Cane Corso. When he passed, I was devastated. So, my husband surprised me with Bane to help me heal."

"So both these dogs, Bowser and Bane, have been at your office while you're with clients?"

"If I was there, they were there."

"You have even brought Bane to my office, correct?"

"Yes, sir."

"Why do you do that? Bring Bane literally everywhere with you?"

"He is a part of my therapy program. It has been proven that dogs are great for helping in the healing process when trained correctly."

"Even your own personal therapy?"

"Yes."

"Tell us more about that, please."

"I was diagnosed with depression and anxiety at sixteen years old. When I was twenty-five, I was diagnosed with PTSD. Bowser could, and Bane can, sense the onset of my panic attacks before I even do and help me through them."

"How so?"

"He gets my attention, so I focus on him. He whines, barks, plays, lays on me—that sort of thing. The more I focus on him, the calmer I get."

"Does he do that with any of your clients?"

"Yes, with their or their parents' permission. They all love him."

"You said you were diagnosed with PTSD. Why were you diagnosed with that?"

I take a deep breath before I answer. "I was severely abused as a child. My ex-stepdad and his son would verbally, mentally, and physically abuse me. It wouldn't be anything for me to have fat lips, bloody noses, fractured ribs, and bruises."

"How long did that last?"

"Eighteen years, but it didn't get severe until I was fourteen and lasted until I was twenty-two."

"Do you know why they did this to you or have any idea why?"

"They wanted to control me and used fear to try. I was never scared and couldn't be controlled. Jack wanted his dad's approval, so he did things to get it, no matter what it was he had to do."

"Objection!" the prosecuting attorney yells. "Neither are here to counter her assumptions on how they thought or felt!"

I turn to the young attorney. "Fine, I will rephrase it for you," I say before the judge can say anything. "Do you want my professional opinion then?" raising one eyebrow at him. I hear my brother snicker from the crowd. The judge gives him a 'knock it off' look.

"Well, prosecutor? Do you want her professional opinion and her to rephrase the answer?"

"I will ask when I cross-examine her, so it can wait."

"Fair enough, scratch that last question and let's continue," the judge states, nodding to my attorney.

"Let's jump to the day in question," he asks me, my full focus back on him. "What happened that day, Mrs. Garrison?"

I go through the story of that day in full detail, leaving nothing out. When I finish, I am on edge and my anxiety is in full swing. I need Bane. *Stay professional, Anna,* I think to myself.

"So you were defending yourself from a man who harassed you, tried to kidnap your child, and tried to kill you?"

"That is correct."

"Bane saved you then?"

"I would be dead if not for Bane, yes."

"No further questions."

# PIECE BY PIECE

I try to relax as much as I can, looking at Rafe to help ground myself. I take slow, deep breaths while not losing eye contact with him. I barely notice the young prosecuting attorney standing in front of me. When I do, I am instantly defensive. *I know this is his job and people get this way with me in mine, but his arrogance due to his age and lack of experience rolls off him like a thick fog.*

"Anna—" he starts.

"It is Dr. Garrison," I retort.

That catches him off guard, and he looks nervous and embarrassed but quickly recovers.

"My apologies, Dr. Garrison. You had stated you were beaten for eighteen years by Bud, correct?"

"Yes."

"In all those years, no one found out? No one questioned any of it?"

"I tried since I was four. He was very narcissistic and good with his words; he would make me out to be a liar or dramatic."

"That must have been upsetting?"

"Well, yes."

"So upsetting that you planned to kill him for years?"

"Objection! We are here for Jack's death. Bud's was ruled self-defense and was closed years ago. No need to question her again on it," my attorney practically yells. I can see his neck and face are beet red with anger.

"Keep your questions relevant to this trial, attorney," the judge warns.

"Yes, sir," the prosecuting attorney says with sarcasm. If the judge heard it, he ignored it. *This kid is playing for the cameras. Little shit.*

"Dr. Garrison, you stated the worst of the abuse was from ages fourteen to twenty-two, correct?"

"Yes."

"What happened at fourteen to make this 'abuse'"—he uses air quotes—"worse?"

*Fuck,* I think to myself. "I got a boyfriend he did not like. He got Jack involved."

"You're telling me that the abuse got worse because of some high school crush?"

"Boyfriend, not a crush. A crush is something you kids say about someone you don't have the balls to talk to," I say, mirroring the sarcastic tone he gave the judge.

He clears his throat. "Why? What about the boyfriend made it worse and got Jack involved?"

For the first time, I look at the crowd. What I am about to say, I want to say while looking them in the eyes—all of them. The eyes I land on are the most beautiful blue eyes I have ever seen, and they are staring at me, hard. *Oh, fuck,* I think. Still tall and broad-shouldered, he seems to fill the room just by being here. Still blonde, still with piercing blue eyes that look right through me. He is all grown up, no longer the boy I knew. After twenty years, he is here, right in front of me. He is more beautiful now than back then.

"Christian," I whisper.

"Dr. Garrison? I need you to speak up; we can't hear you."

"His name was Christian, the boyfriend. He was more than that to me. I loved him, and Bud knew it, used it against me."

"And how did he do that, Doctor?"

"Bud had a government job, which means he knew a lot of people. He told me if I didn't dump Christian and make it seem like I wanted to end it, then he would have Christian pulled over and they would—" I copy his quotation gestures—"'find' cocaine in his car and that he would make sure he rotted in jail for it. I was to make sure I made Christian hate me."

"So, making you dump your high school boyfriend made the abuse worse? How did Jack play into it?"

"I told Bud he was full of shit. A week later, he had a 'friend' come to the house, and they brought Christian up in front of me. His friend confirmed that it could happen whenever Bud said to. That's when I knew Bud was serious, so I dumped Christian and made sure he hated me. To make sure I didn't talk to Christian and tell him everything, Bud had Jack follow me a lot. If I even looked in Christian's direction at school, Jack would run back to his daddy and tell him, then I would get beaten."

"So why did he hate this kid so much?"

## PIECE BY PIECE

I take a deep breath and look the attorney dead in his eyes. "Are you asking me for my professional opinion now or my assumption?"

The crowd laughs, and the attorney goes red.

"Order!" the judge yells, hitting his gavel on the desk.

"Your professional opinion is fine, Doctor," the attorney says, still red in the face.

*Rookie,* I think. I take another deep breath and find Christian again. Here I go, no holding back, time to tell all. I see his mom sitting next to him, tears streaking her face. *I could kill him again just for making her cry. Mom,* I think. She nods at me as if reading my mind.

"Bud knew Christian was my weakness. Christian intimidated him, as he did a lot of people. If I had Christian in my life, then Bud had no control. I was safe with Christian, for the first time in my whole life. Bud couldn't handle that, and Jack wanted to make Daddy happy. They wanted me to break," the tears fall from my eyes, I ignore them and keep going, "If Jack told him that he saw us together, even if he was lying, I got beaten. Jack liked when I got beaten. The worst beating I got was after I came back from visiting Christian at college."

"Why was that the worst?"

"Because before I left I dared him to hit me so I could show Christian and tell him everything. When I came back and Bud knew I wasn't going to tell him, he beat me to the point I ended up in the hospital."

The whole courtroom is quiet except for the sniffles from those crying. No one says a word.

"Is that what caused you to break? How they used your love for him against you?"

"Yes."

"That is why you killed Bud?"

"Objection!"

"There is a reason for the question, Your Honor, in regard to this case."

"Get to it then," the judge demands.

"Doctor, you reached your breaking point over a boy, ending up in you killing Bud in 'self-defense.' How did Jack take that?"

"Not good."

"So Jack confronted you after that hearing and ended up in jail?"

"Yes, he shot me."

"So when he got out, you had your dog kill him?"

He is trying to piss me off, and it works.

"After Jack stalked me and my family, tried to—" *Doctor, that's not—* I cut him off from trying to stop me, raising my voice into an authoritative one I use with clients when I need to.

"—tried to kidnap my daughter! He came to my house, broke in, had a gun. Bane was locked up in the garage. We fought, me for my fucking life! Bane knew I needed him, he broke out the garage window and saved my life."

"So you didn't signal him to kill Jack?"

"After Jack tried to shoot me again? Yes, I did, or have you not seen the video?"

"I have seen it, why did you not let the police handle it?"

"They were not there yet, and Jack would never stop. He wanted me and everything I love dead. I did what I had to do to protect myself and my family, and that includes Bane."

"So how do we know Bane is not a danger to society? To your patients?"

"Do you want to meet him and decide for yourself?"

"A dangerous dog who kills on command? No, thank you."

I shrug, "Your loss, bud. But how will you know if he is a danger or not if you're obviously not going to take my word for it?"

"Have him evaluated by a Dog Behavioral Specialist."

"Of your choosing, I take it?" I ask. He shrugs and nods. "Any 'specialist' you pick will come to the same conclusion, and every patient I've ever had that has met him will tell you he's no danger unless you are hurting me or my kids."

"Do you have those patients to testify on his behalf?"

"Give me the lunch hour, and they will all be here."

# PIECE BY PIECE

He nods and purses his lips. "Okay, bring him in. Muzzled. If Your Honor is okay with it?"

The judge looks back and forth between us. "I will allow it."

## CHAPTER 35

I stay in my seat through the lunch break. It's agreed that Rafe will bring Bane into the courtroom when instructed to. I have a whole damn hour to wait. Wait and let my anxiety grow worse than it was. I don't talk to anyone, except my lawyer.

"Are you okay?" my attorney asks quietly.

"He is here," is all I can say.

"Who?" He looks around, confused.

"Christian."

"The boyfriend from when you were a kid?"

"Yup, him and his mom."

He lets out a low whistle through his teeth. "I'm guessing you had no idea they would be here?"

I shake my head, looking down at my hands. I hold back the tears; I've cried enough.

"Focus on Bane, okay? You just need to prove to them that he's the greatest dog ever like I know he is."

They call court to order as the judge takes his place in front. "Okay, counselor, let's get this over with," he says, looking irritated. I can't tell if he's irritated about me or the fact we have to do this with Bane because he knows Bane is no threat. "Dr. Garrison?" I look up to the judge who is speaking to me.

"Yes, sir?"

"When the dog comes in, please stay in your seat and only react if asked to. Do you understand?"

"Yes, sir."

The doors open, and Rafe walks in with Bane. The muzzle makes him look mean, and it breaks my heart. Bane whines and searches the room, further breaking my heart. The tears start to fall silently.

"Shhh, Bane, it's okay," Rafe whispers to him as they approach the front of the courtroom. I can't look at Bane; I'll lose it, so I focus on Rafe. Bane sees me and tries to come toward me, and Rafe has to pull him back.

"Mr. Garrison, do you have a hold on that dog?" the judge asks Rafe. Bane barks, and I hear a few gasps from the crowd.

"Yes, sir, he just wants his true owner, sir. Bane, sit," Rafe commands. Bane sits, staring at me.

The judge turns to the prosecuting attorney. "Well?"

The guy looks terrified. I'm thinking it's an act, but also that he's a wimp. "Bane?" he asks. Bane doesn't move but starts barking at him. He retreats back to his table. I roll my eyes.

The judge huffs out an annoyed sigh. "Mr. Garrison, control him now!"

"He wouldn't act like this if he could be with his owner. I told you that!" Rafe snaps at the judge.

The judge looks at the prosecuting attorney. "Well, counsel, can he go to his true owner?"

The young attorney nods, and Rafe drops the leash. Gasps erupt again, and I stand. "Bane, come."

Bane bolts for me, and I raise my hand. "Halt." Bane stops and sits, completely focused on me.

"You're gonna grab his leash, right?" the prosecuting attorney asks, looking scared.

No one else says a word, not even the judge. I let out a low whistle to get Bane's attention fully on me.

"Down," I command. Bane lays down. I look at the judge, waiting for more instructions.

"Now what?" I ask. The judge looks at the prosecuting attorney. "Well, now what?"

He looks at me, not sure what to do next, so I take over. "He will not move until I tell him to. He won't listen to anyone but me, not you, not my husband, not the bailiff, no one but me."

My lawyer stands up. "Take his muzzle off."

"No way! He killed a man! He is a bomb waiting to go off!" the prosecuting attorney practically cries.

# PIECE BY PIECE

I look at Bane, stick out my tongue, and cross my eyes at him. He rolls to his back and kicks his feet like a puppy. The crowd, including the judge, laughs. "Some danger," the judge says. "Take off his muzzle; he is no threat."

Rafe steps forward and takes it off Bane. Then he takes off his leash.

"Your honor, I don't think this is a good idea," the prosecuting attorney says.

I step forward and pet Bane. "You wanted to see if he was a danger to the community. Unless you're hurting me or my family, he isn't, obviously." I walk back to my chair, and Bane follows, where my attorney pets him in front of everyone. Bane then lays at my feet, watching me intently.

"Okay, are we done with the dog show? Or do you want to see what other tricks she has for him?" the judge asks the prosecuting attorney.

"It is clear that Dr. Garrison is in full control of that dog and that he is no danger to anyone," my attorney chimes in.

"Do you have anything else, Counselor?" the judge asks.

## PIECE BY PIECE

The prosecuting attorney, looking defeated, sits down. "No, sir."

"Good, Dr. Garrison, you and your dog are released, free and clear of all charges against you both. This was a clear case of self-defense. I wish you both the best."

I look at my attorney, who is smiling at me. "It's all over, Anna. You both can go home."

Bane stands on his hind legs and waves at the judge with both paws. The crowd and the judge laugh. I turn to Rafe and hold him tight. "Let's go home, love."

I hug my mom, dad, and brother before we turn to go. The cameras and news anchors are on me instantly. "Anna! Bane! Can we get a picture? Can you say a few words?"

Rafe rolls his eyes. "Damn dog." I laugh. I grab the muzzle and set it on the prosecuting attorney's table, right in front of him. He says nothing, and we walk out.

We get to the parking lot, fighting through the cameras and people.

"I should have kicked that attorney's ass for putting you both through that!" My dad says, wrapping his arm around my shoulder and giving me a squeeze.

"Thanks, Dad, but I think he learned his lesson."

"Anna?" I hear from behind me. It takes me a minute to find who said it.

"Christian," I whisper as I find him just behind me.

"Oh shit," my brother says.

We lock eyes, and I am that fourteen-year-old girl again. I look beside him and see his mom, who is in tears. I run to her arms. "Hi, Momma." We hug so tight I can't breathe, and I don't care.

"Oh, my sweet girl! I am so proud of you, but we have so much to discuss!" she says, laughing and crying.

"Yes, we do," Christian says in a voice I know means he is pissed. *That has not changed.*

"Diane!" my mom exclaims as she takes my place to hug her. Bane positions himself between Christian and me. Rafe then takes my hand and steps forward, his stance protective. Despite being only half Christian's size, I know my Rafe doesn't care about the size difference.

"I can only assume you are Christian?" Rafe asks, his voice low and defensive. Christian nods. Rafe looks down at me, then back to Christian. "And I can assume you are wanting to discuss things with MY wife?" Christian doesn't flinch; he just nods again.

My brother then steps between them, "She has been through a lot, bro, so if you're here to start trouble, I'm your huckleberry." I roll my eyes.

My brother is the same size as Christian, and they are toe to toe. "She has proven she can handle herself, hasn't she?" Christian asks my brother and Rafe.

"I wasn't there when she grew up. If I had been, those two fuckers would not exist, and NO ONE would ever hurt her," my brother states, taking another step toward Christian, though there wasn't much room to begin with.

Christian doesn't move or blink. "If I had known this back then, those two fuckers wouldn't have existed either," he says, looking past my brother and Rafe at me. His eyes are cold yet soft.

## PIECE BY PIECE

"Oh boys, that's enough," my dad says from behind me, Rafe, and my brother. "Everybody's watching, kids." The cameras and crowd have closed in around us.

Rafe turns to me. "What do you want, Anna?"

I sigh. "I want this all over with, and it can't happen until everything is settled. I want all of this behind me, behind us," I whisper to him.

He nods and turns back to Christian. "Our home is plenty big enough, and no outsiders to get in the way," he says, motioning to the cameras. "You both are welcome to come out and stay as long as needed to get this taken care of."

Christian nods, and Momma O'Brion hugs Rafe. "Thank you!" Rafe gives her a small smile and nods. We then head to our vehicles.

"Anna! Anna! Is that Christian?" a reporter yells. "How does your husband feel about him being here?" another chimes in.

We climb into the Jeep and leave, Rafe nearly hitting a few reporters as we exit the parking lot. "Oops," he says, grinning at me.

# PIECE BY PIECE

The ride home is quiet, with nothing being said. I keep looking at Rafe, but his face gives nothing away. "Rafe?" I ask him. He doesn't take his eyes off the road. "What is it?" I say a little louder.

"Are you fucking kidding me, Anna?" Rafe shouts. I flinch and fall back into my seat. "What is it?" he mocks. "You almost die, then have to go through that bullshit court hearing, the press is up all our asses, and to top it off, your ex from high school and his mom show up and now he wants to 'talk,' and you're okay with this! How the fuck do you think I feel?"

"You could have said no, Rafe! You invited them to the house!" I snap back.

"What was I supposed to do, Anna? How would that have looked to you, him, the press?" he grits out.

"So you did it to make yourself look good, and fuck how you felt? Seriously, Rafe? Don't you trust me?"

"Honestly, I did. Till he came along. I can see it in both your faces."

"That was twenty fucking years ago, Rafe! I had no clue he would even be here! I don't even know why he is here! And for you to say you 'did' trust me and not that you 'do' pisses me off and hurts!"

"You still love him! I can see it in your face!"

"I love you, you fucking jackass!"

"Not in the way you love him." His voice gets quieter with each response.

Mine gets louder, "I was a kid! Fourteen years old! I didn't know what love was! Not until I found God and he gave me you!"

Rafe gives me a sideways glance, "I don't like this, Anna."

"Yeah, well, I didn't add it to my to-do list either."

"Then why do it?"

"I need to get this all out and then put it behind me. Plus, I've really missed his mom, really bad. She is the mom I always wanted. I love my mom very much, but Momma O'Brion never judged me or turned her back on me, not once. She is a big part of why I am the way I am now."

Rafe nods, "I know she is, Anna, you've told me many times."

## PIECE BY PIECE

We pull into our driveway. My parents and brother are in the car behind us. Christian and his mom are behind them. Rafe looks out his side mirror, "I guess he does drive a Ford, so I should know better than to think you'd be into that." He grins at me. "You're an idiot." I laugh and give him a kiss.

I get out of the Jeep and Bane tumbles out as I open his door. The girls and my father-in-law come out of the house. "Bane! You're alive!" They both scream, running to hug him. They hug me next, then Rafe.

"I knew they wouldn't kill him!" Dee exclaims.

"Me too!" Jessie adds.

"Where are my favorite soldiers?" my brother yells, picking both girls up.

"I'm not a soldier, Uncle Justin!" Dee protests.

Justin looks at me and grins. "Okay, Princess Dee."

Christian and his mom walk up, and Jessie hides behind Rafe. Dee, on the other hand, steps between me and Christian, looking like she's squaring off. "Who are you two?" Dee demands.

# PIECE BY PIECE

"Dee! Be nice," I scold her.

Mrs. O'Brion waves me off, "I'm Mrs. O'Brion, and this is my son, Christian," she introduces to Dee.

Dee eyes Christian up and down. "My mom has pictures of you, ma'am, but not him."

"Dee, your mom said to be nice," Rafe chimes in now.

Dee shrugs. "Just saying."

Rafe grabs her by the shoulder, steering her towards the house. "Let's go inside so they can talk."

"You're leaving her alone, with 'him'!" Dee snaps at Rafe.

"Who is the parent, kid?" Rafe retorts, walking into the house.

Justin laughs. "She is all you, sister."

I roll my eyes. "Don't I know it."

He squeezes my shoulder and follows Rafe and the girls inside, meeting Rafe's dad at the door. They immediately talk military.

## PIECE BY PIECE

"Want me to show you around so they can talk?" my mom offers to Mrs. O'Brion.

"Sure!" she says excitedly, and they walk off.

Alone with Christian now, besides Bane, he looks at me. "So?" he asks. *I am internally freaking out.*

"So, do you want to go for a walk? I have a running trail right over there," I suggest, pointing to the trail.

"Sure."

I whistle for Bane to follow, and we start for the trail.

"So, how is life?" I ask when we get out of sight of everyone. I try to mask how nervous I am.

"Oh no, Anna. No small talk. Tell me what the fuck happened back then and how it came to the shit with Jack," his voice is stern.

I sigh. "Fine." I take a deep breath and let it out slowly before I begin. "What all do you want to know?"

"Everything."

"You have that much time?"

## PIECE BY PIECE

"Not funny, Anna."

"Alright, alright," I start to tell him everything, from start to finish. We walk at a slow pace and when I finish, we are at the top of the ridge. I can't look at him; I focus on the view, tears streaming down my face. *Damn it, why am I crying?* He is quiet.

After what seems like forever, he finally speaks. "Why didn't you tell me, Anna?"

I turn to face him, not hiding the pain and hurt anymore. "When would I or could I have told you, Christian? I couldn't tell you."

"Why?" Christian presses for an answer.

"If I had told you when we were kids, fourteen and sixteen years old, what would or could you have done?" I respond.

"I would have killed them both," he says flatly.

"Exactly. They ruined my life, both of them. I couldn't let you ruin yours."

"That wasn't your choice to make, Anna."

I nod, resigned. "Maybe not, but I made it, so here we are." I shrug, my arms spreading out to my sides, then falling to smack against my thighs. The pain is like a sharp memory, revisiting the agonies of my youth.

"Then why didn't you tell me when you came out to visit me at school?" Christian continues, his voice tightening.

I laugh, though it's hollow, turning back to look out over the ridge. "Right, as if you would have believed me. You had your mind made up about me long before that." Silence stretches between us. I wipe my eyes, finding strength returning to me. "I know what you thought of me back then, how you felt about me."

"Oh yeah? And what's that, Anna?"

I close my eyes, the words weighing heavily on me. *I do not want to do this, but I know I need to.* Bane nudges my hand, and I ruffle his ears, drawing a deep breath before I reply. "I broke up with you. I became a drunk and, according to everyone, a slut. You found me gross, dramatic, stupid—a mistake, but your plaything when you were bored with whatever girl was around. You hated me and made sure I knew it. Oh, and I knew it. Got that message loud and clear."

"I didn't know the truth, Anna."

## PIECE BY PIECE

I glance over my shoulder at him, offering a weak smile. "I know you didn't."

"So you loved me that much? Enough to protect me even if it meant losing you?"

I remain silent.

"Anna, please," his voice softens and becomes calmer.

I shake my head, struggling to hold back the sobs caught in my throat.

"What kind of love is that? How could you even love me like that? We weren't together very long and then off and on after. I was, am, nothing special."

Again, I shake my head, unable to voice my feelings.

"Anna, we need to get this out in the open. Clear the air. Just tell me what you're thinking and feeling so we can resolve this."

I wipe my nose and eyes on my sweater sleeve, covering my face with both hands, still shaking my head. Suddenly, I feel two big, strong arms wrap around me, pulling me into his chest. I begin to sob uncontrollably, Bane looking up at me, confused.

## PIECE BY PIECE

Christian squeezes me tighter and whispers in my ear that it's okay.

I jerk away from him. "No! No, it is not okay, Christian! You have no clue what it was like!" My anger builds, Bane, trying to nudge me. "You have no idea what it was like to make that choice at our age and then live with it this long! To watch someone you loved grow to hate you and then see them with someone else. To hold that secret and be strong all the time. To pretend that you were something that you weren't so the truth wouldn't be found out. To hide how you feel and how much you love someone! To know that they are the most beautiful person you ever saw and compare anyone who tried to come close to them, knowing they fall short. To know that the only person who made you feel safe and loved hated you." I don't stop, I let it all out. "I was a toy to you, a piece of shit that you discarded when you were done and you can't blame them because you made sure they thought of you that way to hide the truth and protect them. That everything you ever wanted in life was right there and you had to act like it wasn't."

He steps towards me and I put my hands up, "Don't, Christian. Let me finish." He stops, his pain evident on his face. "You were everything to me, Christian. Fucking everything! You were the hero in the books I read, the movies I watched." I laugh,

## PIECE BY PIECE

"I used to think you were it for me and I messed it up. I used to imagine the what-ifs, what if I had made a different choice and told you. What if we had stayed together? Got married and had kids? And you know what I realized? That I loved you way more than you ever loved me. God knew I had a future and you were not part of it. That love I thought I had with you was nothing in comparison to what I found in Rafe. He would never hurt me, even if I hurt him. He is a safety I can't explain. He is what I wanted you to be and you weren't."

Christian shoves his hands in the pockets of his jeans and stays quiet. He looks at the ground, then off the ridge, then back at me. "Anna, I did love you, but we were also kids." I nod. "I can't tell you where we would be had things been different. All I do know is that life gave us all the cards we needed to play to get to where we are now. I am truly sorry for hurting you."

I nod and take a deep breath. "We should head back." He nods, and we start back to the house. The walk is quiet. I fully understand now that my love was really one-sided. I silently thank God for it because if he had loved me as much as I loved him back then, I wouldn't have what I have now. God knew what I needed. I see Rafe standing on our deck and silently thank God again.

## PIECE BY PIECE

We say our goodbyes as Christian and his mom get ready to leave. Rafe takes my hand. "Everything okay?" he asks.

I look at him and feel the mutual love we share. I wrap my arms around his waist, leaning my head against his chest. "Everything is perfect," I say as we watch them drive away.

Rafe kisses me, and I return it with a deeper, more passionate one. "Ewwww! Gross!" Dee whines from behind us. Rafe and I burst out laughing.

Later, I walk onto my deck, the cool wind brushing my face. My dad is sitting there with a sweet tea and Jack Daniels mixed drink in his hand. "Can I have some?" I ask, taking the seat next to him.

He hands me the glass. "You doing okay, baby girl?" I'm in my thirties, but I will never tire of hearing him call me that.

"Yeah, Dad, I am," I reply, taking a big swig of his drink.

"You got the closure you needed then?"

"Yeah, I did," I say, nodding and taking another drink before handing it back to him.

# PIECE BY PIECE

"That part of your life is now over, Anna. Never again do you have to worry or be scared about them."

"It feels like a weight has been lifted, you know? Like I finally got all the pieces in place."

He stands and stretches. "I love you, baby girl, and I'm very proud of you."

"Thank you, Dad."

He pulls out his phone and plays "Piece by Piece," our song. "Dance with me?" he says as he sets his phone down and holds out his hand. I take it as we begin to dance. I glance through the window of my house and see Rafe, my girls, and Bane all playing on the floor in the living room. I thank God again and couldn't imagine a better way to end that chapter of my life and start a new one.

# PIECE BY PIECE

www.ingramcontent.com/pod-product-compliance
Lightning Source LLC
LaVergne TN
LVHW020423070526
838199LV00003B/253